Stanly opened his eyes. His head throbbed, his throat was parched, and his stomach grumbled uncontrollably. He drew the back of his right hand across his forehead and then let it drop dejectedly back on the bed. As he did so, however, his hand brushed against something soft and warm. . .

NEVER MARRY A VIRGIN, STANLY

by

David Mark Rhodes

APOLLO BOOKS

Woodbridge, Conn.

This story is most gratefully dedicated to my friend Rollie who was there when I needed him — and a few times when I didn't, to Randi, one hell of a really fine broad, and to my brother Dane, simply because he has always wanted a book dedicated to him.

Covery Art
by
Gregory Harris
Printed in the United States of America

You laughed and told me
There were no dragons or ogres
Then gently took me by the hand
And led me to their lair.

Chapter I

"I don't want to be drafted," Stanly Allen said aloud.

Hiram Burroughs glanced up from the term paper he was typing. "What did you say?"

"I don't want to be drafted," Stanly repeated.

"What are you talking about?"

"The draft. I don't want to be drafted."

"Are you feeling all right, Stan?"

"No."

"What's the matter?"

"I don't want to be drafted."

"You keep saying that."

"That's because I don't want to be drafted."

Hiram Burroughs shook his head sadly, not so much at his roommate's distress as at his own for not being able to ignore him, and pushed himself away from the typewriter where he was working.

"Look, Stan, in the first place you are here at Midwestern on an art scholarship aren't you?"

Stanly nodded half-heartedly.

"And you've got your student deferment don't you?"

"Yes."

"Then what the hell are you worrying about the draft for? Your number's not that low so you're safe for at least four years."

"I'm going to lose my scholarship and my deferment," Stanly said blankly.

"What?"

Stanly pointed at his roommate's term paper. "How many pages have you got?"

Hiram looked back at his work and quickly shuffled through his neatly typed labor. "About twenty-five. Why?"

Stanly grabbed a handful of blank papers off of his desk and threw them into the air.

"That's how many I've written," he said as the white sheets floated like giant snowflakes toward the floor.

"You stupid ass," Hiram said wrinkling his brow, "It's due at the end of next week."

"I know."

"Why haven't you done anything then?"

"I want to be an artist."

"What?"

"I want to be an artist. Why should I have to write a term paper on the irrigation canals of Colombia, Venezuela, and the Guianas?"

"Are you crazy?"

"Why should I have to write a term paper on the irrigation canals of Colombia, Venezuela, and the Guianas?" Stanly repeated, "What good will it do me? What do I care if they have ten canals or ten thousand! It's ridiculous for me to have to do it.

"I want to be an artist. I want to create beauty; something that will exist, something that will last and be admired hundreds of years after I'm dead and gone. Something that people can look at and point to and say, 'see that? Stanly Allen did that.' I don't want to write about canals. Why should I have to?"

"So you don't flunk out of college," Hiram said with that forthright sensibility of his which so many people mistook for sarcasm.

"That's right. My whole life depends on Venezuelan canals; their construction and purpose. Whether I stay in college or not will depend on whether I get a passing grade in history 101. If I flunk this paper I get kicked out of college. I lose my scholarship, I lose my deferment, and I become eligible for the draft again. Just because I want to be an artist, and not a historian or a writer of Venezuelan canals."

"I've never seen you like this before. Besides, you won't get kicked out of college just for flunking one class."

"I'm not flunking just one class."

Hiram stared questioningly at Stanly. "How many?"

"Five."

"Five!" Hiram ejaculated.

Stanly nodded, keeping his eyes positioned on the floor.

"My God, Stan, how many classes are you taking?"

"Six."

"Six! Dammit, Stan, how can you be flunking five classes?"

"I work at it," Stanly said in a monotone.

"Nobody flunks five classes, Stan. Especially not you."

Stanly kept his eyes on the floor.

"Stan?"

"I'm getting an A in art," he said limply.

Hiram ran his long thin fingers through his straight straw colored hair, scratched his long thin nose and then pushed his black horn-rimmed glasses back on the bridge of his nose. "You had a four point all through high school."

"I know."

"What are you going to do?"

"I don't know. I just don't care any more. These are stupid classes they're making me take. I just don't care about them."

" You're in trouble, Stan," Hiram finally said.

"I know."

"So, what happens now?"

"I don't know. I was never put in a position like this before. I don't want to fight! I don't want to kill! I don't want to be drafted! And I don't want to write about Venezuelan canals! I want to be an artist, that's all."

"There's going to be a lot of things that you don't want to do."

"Why?"

"What?"

"Why?"

"Because that's just the way life is."

"Why is that the way life is? Why not change it?"

"You better get busy on that term paper."

"No."

Hiram shook his head again and returned to his typing.

"Hiram?" Stanly said after a few minutes of silence, save for the click clicking of the typewriter.

"What!" Hiram shouted at the interruption.

"Nothing."

Hiram pushed himself away from the typewriter once again.

"Stanly?" he asked calmly.

"What?"

"What did you want?"

"Nothing."

"You sure?"

"I'm sure."

"You hungry?"

"No."

Without warning, the loudest, most erotic, most vulgar music suddenly ripped apart the walls of their dorm room. Hiram grabbed for his ears in a futile attempt to protect them from the sanity-shattering sound, then threw down his hands, his long thin fingers tightening into a balled fist, save for the middle finger which protruded out straight in a gesture of disgust.

"Damn him!" he shouted above the noise.

Hiram knocked his chair over as he raced to the far wall and began beating on it. "Far Out! Far Out, do you hear me! If you don't turn down that goddamn stereo I'm going to kill you! Far Out!"

The music faded into abrupt silence almost as quickly as it had begun, leaving only Hiram's continued swearing to be heard.

Stanly picked up one of the papers he had thrown on the floor. He looked at its emptiness for a moment, and then took out a pencil and passively began to sketch Hiram's portrait.

"One of these days I'm going to kill that goddamned Far Out if he doesn't keep his fucking stereo turned down," Hiram said. "Stanly?"

"What?"

"You going to homecoming?"

"What?"

"Are you going to homecoming?"

"Homecoming?"

"Yeah. Are you going?"

"No."

"How about the dance? Are you going to that?"

"No."

"Why not?"

Stanly didn't answer. Instead, he handed Hiram the sketch he had done. Hiram looked at the paper in approval.

"That's very good."

"I know," Stanly said quietly.

"You ought to be an artist."

"Why couldn't I paint a mural?"

"What?"

"I don't want to be a historian. I want to be an artist. Why couldn't I paint a mural instead of writing a term paper?"

"Why don't you go to homecoming?"

Stanly stared at the floor for a long while. "When is it?" he finally asked.

"About three weeks; that's still plenty of time to get a date, and you'll still be in school; grades won't come out for a couple of weeks after that."

"You going?"

"Hell, yeah."

"You got a date?"

"Not yet."

"Oh."

Stanly got down on his knees and began picking up the papers he had thrown on the floor.

"You been out on a date since you started college?" Hiram asked.

"No."

"That's almost two months."

"I know."

"I think you ought to go to homecoming. It will take your mind off of the draft and term papers and being an artist."

"No."

"Why not for chrissake?"

"I don't want to go."

Stanly reached for the last paper, and then dumped the entire mess on his desk.

"You seen the Queen candidates, Stan?" Hiram asked.

"Queen candidates?"

"For homecoming."

"No."

"They're fine. There's finally some half-way decent ones to choose from this year."

"Have you decided who you're going to take?" Stanly suddenly asked.

"Not yet — Tracy Williams is one of them."

"Tracy Williams is one of them?"

"The biggest broad in this school, Tracy Williams, is one of the Queen candidates."

"Oh."

"Wouldn't it be funny if she got elected queen?"

Stanly took his wire-rimmed glasses off and wiped the lenses with his shirt tail.

"Why would it be funny?" he asked, putting his glasses back on.

"Because she'd have to go to the homecoming dance without a date — or with her brother."

"Why would she have to do that?"

"You know that animal she's been going with."

"Gunther?"

"He's in Nebraska."

"So?"

"So, with him gone there's nobody to take her. At least I don't think there's anybody around here who's stupid enough to do something like that."

"Stupid enough?"

"Stan, Gunther may be a kindergarten drop out, but he's an animal, right? If he got back from Nebraska and found out that someone had taken his girl out, he'd kill whoever it was that had done it."

"Oh."

Stanly was quiet for a long minute. "Why's he in Nebraska?"

"Gunther?"

Stanly nodded.

"I don't know. I think his brother shot somebody there or something. But I figure he's not particularly worried about anyone moving in on Tracy while he's gone. Wouldn't it be a waste though; all that beauty, the beast away, and no one to take advantage of it."

"Yeah," Stanly said softly to himself.

"You going to write your term paper, Stan?"

"No!"

For the next week, Stanly attended classes regularly and visited his draft board information center daily. Usually his trips to class were sheer agony and his visits to the center only saddened and depressed him.

"What did they have to say at the old draft board today?" Hiram asked as Stanly came into the dorm late that Friday afternoon.

"They recommended I move to Canada," Stanly said blankly.

"Have you done your term paper on Venezuelan canals yet?"

"No."

"It's due next Friday."

"I know."

"Why don't you just do the paper, then you wouldn't have to worry about the draft."

"No. You just don't understand."

"Understand what, Stan? That you're going to flunk out of college. I understand that all right. You're the one that doesn't seem to understand."

"It's not that! It's not just the paper, it's the whole principle behind it. I want to be an artist. That's all. I don't want to write, I want to draw. If I had been asked to draw a picture, and then have the decision of whether I stay in college or not rest on how good I did it, I could see that. But I wasn't. I was told to write a paper. I'm not a writer. I don't want to be a writer. Yet, my whole life depends on how well I can write."

"You're crazy," Hiram said.

Stanly simply stared at him in silence.

Hiram shook his head, "You're crazy," he repeated. "You going to the peace rally tomorrow?"

"What peace rally?"

"It's in the paper," Hiram said as he tossed Stanly an issue. "A bunch of the resident freaks are holding a demonstration against the war in Viet Nam. And the way you've been acting lately, I thought you'd like to know about it. You ought to fit in real well with all the other draft dodgers on campus."

Stanly ignored the remark; "Where's it going to be?"

"In front of the old music building."

"What time?"

"I think it starts around seven tomorrow morning; or some ungodly hour like that. It's supposed to last all day, unless they get busted by the cops."

"Why would they get busted? What are they going to do?"

"I don't know. I've got nothing to do with it. I have the feeling it's all being run by the mentally insane, and that's why I thought you'd like to know about it. You going?"

"No."

"I've got to get a date," Hiram suddenly said.

"What?"

"Homecoming's in two weeks, and I still haven't got a date."

"Oh."

"You going?"

"To homecoming?"

Hiram nodded.

"No! And I'm not going to the peace rally either!"

The words had no more than left Stanly's mouth when the door flew open and what resembled the apparition of an over-grown elf strutted into the room.

"All right you Marine recruits," It shouted, "You're in the army now, not back at the demonstrations!"

"Get out of here, Spike," Hiram said, "You're not funny."

"You sassing me, boy," Spike continued in his Marine sergeant voice.

"Go on, Spike," Stanly said.

"Just don't give me no shit, boy," Spike said and strode out of the room singing, "I want to be an airborne ranger. I want to live a life of danger. I want to . . . "

"You see that," Stanly said, "It isn't fair. Spike tried to enlist in the Marines but they wouldn't take him. Can you believe that? He wanted to enlist, and they wouldn't take him just because he was too short. I don't want to have anything to do with it; yet they'd draft me just like that," he said snapping his fingers.

As if on cue Far Out's music began shaking loose bits of plaster from the ceiling.

"Damn you, Far Out!" Hiram screamed and suddenly the music stopped. "This place is a zoo," Hiram continued. "I've got to get out of here. Want to go to the game?"

"What game?"

"Don't you ever pay any attention to what's going on around this school? The football game tonight. We're playing Wyoming. It's going to be a big game."

"No. I don't want to go."

"What are you going to do tonight?"

"I don't know."

"Then why don't you go to the game?"

"I don't want to go."

"Why not? It's Friday; no classes tomorrow."

"I just don't want to go."

"Think of the girls."

"What girls?"

"The ones at the game. There's always broads at football games."

Stanly walked into the bathroom.

"Stanly," Hiram called after him.

"What?"

"I'll pay for your ticket," Hiram said.

Stanly came slowly out of the bathroom and shook his head negatively. Then he looked up at Hiram and after a moment's silence. "All right," he said.

Chapter II

"Well, here we are," Hiram said as the guards at the gate frisked him for booze, pot, and bombs, "at Midwestern's most elaborate temple of worship. Five million dollars worth of planned obsolescence. In ten years this entire football stadium will be nothing but a pile of rubble."

"Are you kidding?" Stanly asked as the guards began their inspection tour on him.

Hiram shook his head, "Don't you ever read the paper?"

"No."

"Well, my most literate friend, according to the papers it only cost five million dollars to pay for this stadium; five million of our dollars. That's why your tuition went up. You are paying an extra sixty bucks for athletic fees; whether you go to any events or not. Look at it this way, this is the first game you've gone to this year. And knowing you, it will probably be the last. So, you just paid sixty bucks for this seat. Mighty expensive seat if you ask me. Especially considering that you have to be frisked before you can even get to it."

Stanly stared at him in disbelief.

"Not only that," Hiram continued as he warmed to the subject nearest and dearest his crusading heart, "but this magnificent monstrosity has been here but a single solitary year and has already acquired a crack right down the middle; within ten years the whole thing is supposed to fall apart. Nice, huh? But the best is yet to come. Do you know that this stadium is only used five times a year! Five times in a single year! It's too small for track, the wrong shape for baseball, and you can't bounce a basketball on fake grass. So, Midwestern plays five home games — five football games a year on it, and that's it. Then it is locked up and not used again until next year. That is, if it's still standing next year."

Stanly digested the information and then glanced around at the already packed stadium.

"We'll never find a seat," he said simply.

"We're not here to watch the game anyway," Hiram said, "I didn't pay sixty dollars just to watch a football game."

"We're not?"

"We're here to find me a date for homecoming."

"I'm not going to homecoming," Stanly said.

"Well, I am," Hiram retorted, "Now here's an empty seat," he said taking Stanly by the shoulders and seating him. "You sit here and watch the game, and I'll be back at the half."

"Where are you going?" Stanly demanded.

"To find a date."

"You're leaving me alone?"

"I'll be back at the half," Hiram answered as he started off through the crowd.

"But Hiram. . . " Stanly called out as his roommate disappeared into the throng of people.

Stanly watched the game until someone on the field called time out. Then he got up and started to wander through the stands in search of Hiram.

"All I want to be is an artist," he said to himself, "I didn't even want to come to the game."

"Hello, Stanly," a voice called to him.

Stanly looked down at the bleachers at the sound of his name, and recognized Sheila Reed, a girl he had vaguely known in high school.

"Hi," he finally managed to say.

"I didn't know you were going to Midwestern," Sheila scolded, "Why didn't you tell me? Why I haven't seen you since we graduated."

"Yeah."

"What are you doing now?"

"I'm looking for someone."

"No, I meant in college."

Stanly shook his head. "Nothing."

"What are you majoring in?"

"Art."

"That's nice. . .did you say you were looking for someone?"

Stanly nodded.

"Anyone I know?"

"Hiram Burroughs," Stanly said.

She shook her head. "I don't think I know him."

"A tall thin guy — has blonde hair and wears black horn-rimmed glasses."

"No, I don't know him," she said.

"Down in front!" a number of the spectators whose view was blocked began yelling at Stanly as they pelted him with empty peanut bags and candy wrappers.

Sheila scooted over. "You had better sit down," she cautioned, "They are trying to watch the game."

"Oh, sorry," Stanly said to no one in particular, and sat

down beside her.

"What did you say you were majoring in?"

"Art," Stanly said again.

"That must be exciting."

Stanly nodded absent-mindedly.

"Are you going to homecoming?"

"I don't know."

Stanly was silent, absorbed in his answer. It seemed that everyone in the whole world was concerned with whether he was going to homecoming or not. Stanly glanced at Sheila, her long black hair waving in the slight breeze of the evening silhouetted her extremely pretty features. Stanly sucked in his breath. The football field became a blur. He felt like a matador in front of a charging bull, facing the moment of truth with nothing more than a toothpick.

"Sheila," he finally stammered, "would you like to go to homec-. . .."

"Look!" Sheila suddenly shouted, and pointed toward the football field.

Stanly looked in the direction she had indicated.

A Midwestern player leaped into the air, intercepted a pass, and then raced twenty yards for a touchdown. The Midwestern crowd sent up a series of cheers, and in the distance, a cannon sounded.

"Isn't Larry beautiful," Sheila murmured as the crowd died down to a minimal roar.

"Larry?" Stanly asked.

"Larry Holbrook."

"They all look the same to me," Stanly said, "how do you know that one was Larry Holbrook?"

"Well, I've been going with him long enough to know his number by now. Number twenty-four. You know Larry, we went together in high school, remember? He even had the same number then."

Stanly stared at her for an endless second. "Huh?" he suddenly uttered.

"Is something the matter?"

"No," Stanly said shaking his head, "I've got to be going."

Stanly quickly got up and made his way back to his original seat. He watched the rest of the game by himself until Hiram returned at the half.

"Did you get a date?" Stanly asked as Hiram stopped in front of him.

"Yeah." Hiram smiled smugly.

"You did?"

Hiram nodded and added with a flippant air, "With Malcolm's sister."

"Who?"

"Malcolm's sister."

"Who's Malcolm?"

"You don't know Malcolm?"

Stanly shook his head.

"He's a friend of Far Out's," Hiram said.

"Far Out has friends?"

"Well, he's not really a friend. He's more like a consumer. He's one of Far Out the pill pusher's best buyers."

"He's not a friend of Far Out's — he's a buyer."

"Right."

"And you're going to homecoming with Malcolm's sister."

"That's right."

"Oh."

"You going to homecoming, Stan?"

"No."

Stanly stood up and started for the main exit gate.

"Where you going?" Hiram called after him.

"Home."

"But the game's not over yet."

"Yes, it is," Stanly said.

Chapter III

The next morning, Stanly was up early which was extremely unusual for him, especially on a Saturday. He shaved, dressed, and then tripped over a chair, which woke Hiram up.

"What time is it?" Hiram asked rubbing the sleep from his eyes.

"Seven."

The door exploded inward and Spike the elf bounded in, "All right you Commie pinkos on your feet. It's chow time!"

"Get out of here," Hiram shouted from his bed.

"Don't give me no shit, boy," Spike said lighting a cigar and strolling out of the room, "I don't take lip from no one."

Hiram rubbed the sleep from his eyes, "What are you doing up so early?"

Stanly muttered something under his breath and started out of the room.

"What?" Hiram said, stopping him at the door with his voice.

"I decided to go the peace rally," Stanly said a little louder.

Hiram rolled over on his bed laughing, then sat up straight and serious. "You think it will help end the war?"

"I don't care if it will or not. I don't care if other people have wars or not. If that's their thing, that's fine with me. I just don't want to fight it for them. I want to be an ar. . . "

"I know," Hiram said, "you want to be an artist."

Stanly nodded.

"I thought you said you weren't going to the demonstration," Hiram said blandly, "You don't seem to be overly concerned about ending the war, or bringing the soldiers home."

"I'm not. But if I get drafted, then I'll be one of the soldiers over there that need to be brought home and I'll be very concerned. So, if the only way to keep me from getting drafted is to stop the war, then I'll attend the peace rally."

"You could write your term paper. You still have six days before it's due."

"No."

"Give me a minute," Hiram said, climbing out of bed, "and I'll go with you."

"Why?" Stanly asked suspiciously.

"I've always been attracted by the bizarre. I guess that's why we're such good friends," Hiram smiled.

Stanly and Hiram arrived in front of the old music building shortly after seven thirty. There was already a fairly large crowd gathered around a make-shift stage, listening to a black militant student stutter into a microphone.

"Isn't this fun," Hiram said.

Stanly didn't answer.

"Hey look!" Hiram said, "They're giving out black armbands. You want a black armband, Stan?"

"No."

"It's the latest style for patriotic draft-dodgers!"

"I don't want one."

"I think you'd look real nifty in one."

"No."

Stanly stuck his hands into his pockets, and listened to the speaker. By this time, the speaker had shifted from the black militant, to an English poet, who was reading an assortment of his anti-war poems.

Hiram tapped Stanly on his shoulder.

"Look over there," he said, "Oh man, am I glad I came after all."

Stanly followed Hiram's pointing finger, but all he saw was a massive blur of people.

"What am I supposed to be looking at?" Stanly asked.

"See the blonde?"

Stanly searched the crowd again and then nodded.

"Wait till she turns around. That's Tracy Williams."

"Is it?"

The blonde turned around.

"It is," Hiram said. He waved to her and she waved back.

"You *know* her?" Stanly asked in amazement.

"I met her last night," Hiram said, "she was with Malcolm's sister — they're close friends."

Stanly looked back toward her, and saw that she was approaching them. Stanly began moving back and forth trying desperately to retreat into the comfort of the crowd.

"What are you doing?" Hiram asked.

Suddenly Tracy was upon them.

"Hi!" she said stopping in front of Stanly.

"Hello," Hiram said.

Stanly nodded again, but this time he brought his eyes up to a level even with her breasts; a place where most males, when they met Tracy, had a tendency to focus their attention.

"It might be said that Tracy Williams was well endowed. Of course, it might be said that New York City is a big town — "

Hiram had once told him. Both seemed to Stanly to be understatements once you've seen either first hand.

"I'm Tracy Williams," she said.

"I know," Stanly mumbled, finally reaching her face. Then he gazed into her emerald green eyes, sparkling in the early morning sun, and all the thoughts that were left to his command, for some reason had nothing at all to do with the peace rally, the draft, or term papers.

"I've seen some of your pictures. The ones hanging in the art room," she continued.

Stanly coughed.

"They're very good."

"I know — thank you," Stanly said.

"Isn't this exciting!"

"Yes!" Stanly said instantly, and then wondered what it was that was exciting her; he knew very well what was exciting him.

"Wouldn't it be wonderful," Tracy said, "if enough people could get together like this, all over the United States, and bring our troops home and maybe end the war?"

"Wonderful," Stanly said.

"You don't have an armband!" Tracy suddenly cried.

"What?" Stanly looked down at his arm and shook his head.

"Here, take mine," she said, untying the piece of black cloth from about her own arm and retying it around Stanly's.

"There you are," she said patting his arm lightly.

"Thank you," Stanly mumbled.

"I'll be right back; I want to get another one," she said rushing off.

"I thought you didn't want an armband," Hiram said.

Stanly watched Tracy fade into the crowd.

"That's a real shame," Hiram said.

"What?"

"Tracy."

"What about her?" Stanly demanded.

"That she isn't going to have a date for homecoming."

Stanly was quiet for a minute. "She's going to have a date," he said slowly.

Suddenly the crowd broke into a loud cheer, and began chanting, "End the war! End the war! End the war!"

"What?" Hiram asked, "I couldn't hear you!"

"Love not war!" the crowd screamed, "Love not war! Love not war!"

"I'm going to take her to homecoming," Stanly said softly.

"What did you say?" Hiram asked, cupping his hand by his ear and trying to make out Stanly's words over the roar of the crowd.

"Peace, brother, peace!" someone shouted into the microphone, "Bring our boys home!"

The chant was immediately seized by the crowd. "Peace, brother, peace! Bring our boys home!"

Unexpectantly a siren shattered the sound of the chanting.

"It's the PIGS!" the student who had started the chant said into the microphone, "Sit down, everyone, sit down where you are!"

All around Stanly people dropped to the ground. In a matter of moments, everyone except Stanly had assumed a sitting position.

"Hey, man," someone with a beard who was sitting at Stanly's feet began tugging at his pants cuffs.

"What?"

"Sit down."

Stanly looked around him, then at Hiram who had also taken his place on the ground at the command, and then back at the bearded student.

"Why?"

The bearded student pointed at the circle of police cars, their blue and white colors surrounding them. "The Pigs!" he said in simple explanation.

Stanly glanced at the circle of police cars. From one of them, a tall burly man stepped out, straightened his rumpled trousers, and started toward Stanly, followed by a smaller man who also wore rumpled trousers.

"Damned hippies! They're nothing more than a pack of damned useless garbage — a bunch of rabble rousers!" the big man said to the little one. "You used to be able to just bash them in the head, and drag 'em into the station and book 'em. But since the press has blown it up so big about 'police brutality', now we have to be so damned nice and polite to them."

The little man said nothing as he was still busily engaged in trying to unrumple his trousers so the big one continued with his tirade.

"Hell! That one standing up must be their leader. "We'll talk to him first. C'mon, let's get this over with."

The two men approached Stanly, being careful to step around, and avoid touching each sitting figure.

"I'm officer Rice, campus riot control," the big man said, "here is my badge and credentials," he continued flipping his wallet in front of Stanly's face. "And will you please ask these people to move. They are obstructing entrance to the building."

Although the building, erected in 1887, had been closed down for five years, and not been used for twice that long; and though there were rumors that the building was soon to be demolished because it was considered a firetrap, it was suddenly very important, at least to the police, that the old music building be opened for entrance to the public immediately.

"What?" Stanly asked.

"Please," the little man said, trying to be helpful but pleasant.

Stanly looked from the smaller man back to the larger man, but not knowing what to say, he said exactly that, nothing.

"I take it you're not going to tell them to move," Rice said.

"Tell them to move?" Stanly echoed dumbfoundedly.

"Please?" the little man said again, this time more helpful but less pleasant.

"We're just wasting time with him," Rice said.

Stanly looked at Rice in bewilderment.

"This is your last chance, kid, are you going to tell these people to move?"

"I can't do that," Stanly said honestly.

Officer Rice glanced down at Stanly's black armband and shook his head with disgust. "Do you want to go peacefully or in handcuffs?"

"I don't want to go anywhere at all," Stanly said assuredly.

"You're under arrest," Rice said.

"For what?"

"Disturbing the peace, inciting a riot — "

"No, you don't understand," Stanly said.

" — resisting arrest — "

"No, you don't understand," Stanly said again.

"Handcuff him," Rice said.

Chapter IV

Stanly stared blankly at the stone grey walls of his cell.

"What are you here for?" a soft raspy voice asked.

Stanly turned at the sound. "What?"

Two young men who were occupying the same cell came up beside Stanly. Both were outfitted in what looked like patched rejects of ancient Salvation Army uniforms. Both wore their blond hair long, and the older of the two also supported a thin wispy beard.

"What are you in for?" the younger asked again.

Stanly held his head in his hands, "Inciting a riot, disturbing the peace, and resisting arrest."

"Really?" the bearded one said, "Wow! That's fine! That's really far out."

"What's your name?" the younger one asked.

"Allen; Stanly Allen," Stanly said, closing his eyes and shaking his head remorsefully.

"I'm David Williams," the younger said and pointed at his bearded companion, "This is Joe Hollindorfer."

Stanly opened his eyes, nodded in recognition, and then returned his stare back toward the wall.

"Your name sounds familiar," Joe said, "Do I know you?"

Stanly shrugged.

"Something the matter?" Joe asked.

Stanly looked up at him with an expression of disbelief on his face. "I'm in jail for inciting a riot, disturbing the peace, and resisting arrest; and you ask me if something is the matter. No, no, everything is just fine. Maybe I'll get the electric chair or the gas chamber, and then everything will be just perfect!"

"Hell, we're here for pushing acid. That's worse than what you got. And do we look worried?"

Stanly scratched the tip of his nose with his right forefinger and shook his head.

"You know why?" Joe said with a half-assed grin on his face.

"No," Stanly said.

"Well, I'll tell you why," Joe said, " 'cause we're busting out of here tonight."

"Shut up, Jo Jo, you don't know that we can trust him — besides, he may be a narc."

Joe suddenly grabbed Stanly by the collar with his massive hands and shook him like a terrier would shake a rat.

"You a narc!" Joe shouted.

The force of the action shook Stanly's glasses off of his nose and they dropped to the floor.

"You knocked my glasses off!" Stanly shouted back at Joe.

"You a narc!" Joe shouted again.

"You knocked my glasses off!"

"You a narc!"

"You knocked my glasses off!"

Williams grabbed Joe by the shoulders.

"Let him go, Jo Jo! I was only kidding! Let him go!"

Joe released his grip on Stanly.

"You're not a narc, are you?" Williams said.

"He knocked my glasses off," Stanly said.

"Get his glasses, Jo Jo."

Joe bent down, carefully picked up the glasses, and handed them to Stanly.

"You're not a narc, are you?" Williams repeated.

"I don't even know what that means," Stanly said.

"Liar!" Joe shouted.

"Be quiet Jo Jo. You trying to tell us you don't know what a narc is?"

"That's what I did tell you."

"You've never dropped anything, have you?"

Stanly stared at him blankly.

"He's all right, Jo Jo," Williams said, "He's no narc — narcs are always the first to tell you they're on dope. Narcs are crafty bastards. He's no narc."

"He's all right, Davie?"

"He's all right, Jo Jo."

Stanly sat down on the only piece of furniture in the entire cell, a lone cot, and contemplated suicide.

"I didn't — all I did was stand up at a sit-in."

Williams whistled, "You really got guts, man. Standing up at a sit-in. Wow. That's something. That's really something. You're all right."

Joe, who had been staring for some while at Stanly, continued his concentration for a few seconds longer and then shouted in triumph, "I know who you are!"

Stanly looked up at him in confusion.

"You're the guy that's got all those pictures hung up around the college, ain't ya?"

Stanly nodded and then glanced back up at Joe in disbelief, "You go to college?"

"Only to the demonstrations."

"Allen!" a voice suddenly called, "Stanly Allen!"

"Here," Stanly said as he focused on a uniformed figure in front of the bars of his cell.

"Come on, Allen," the policeman said, "You're free."

"Free?" Stanly repeated.

"Your bail's been paid, so you're free."

The cell door swung open and Stanly started to go out, but then turned back to Williams.

"Is there anything I can do for you?"

Williams shook his head and smiled, "We're fine."

A look of concern came over Stanly's face, "You're not really going to try and break out of here are you?" he whispered under his breath so that the guard wouldn't be able to hear.

"No," Williams said simply.

Stanly looked incredulously at him, "You're not? But Joe said — "

"Jo Jo says anything I tell him. We're not breaking out. My sister will be along in a few hours and bail us out like usual."

"Like usual? Does this happen often?"

"Maybe once or twice a week. This place is getting to be like a second home to us."

Stanly shook his head, "So long," he said.

"Another time," Williams replied.

Stanly finished signing his release papers and then collected his personal items which had been taken from him when he first went in.

"Hiram," Stanly said, "Where did you get the money to bail me out?"

"I borrowed it from Spike and Far Out and Shelly."

Stanly grabbed Hiram by the shoulder, "You're the best friend I've got, Hiram."

Hiram shrugged his shoulders, "You owe Spike and Far Out and Shelly ten bucks apiece."

"And how much do I owe you? How much did you have to spend out of your own pocket. Tell me the truth."

"Nothing," Hiram said simply.

"What?"

"Nothing. I wasn't going to spend my own money on you. I wasn't sure if you could pay me back. That's why I borrowed the money from Spike and Far Out and Shelly."

"Thanks friend, thanks a lot," Stanly said as he stared dejectedly at the ground. "Ten bucks!" he said suddenly, "Ten bucks apiece. That's only thirty dollars. You mean my bail was only thirty dollars!"

"Yeah."

"Thirty dollars," Stanly said slowly, "I thought it would be at least a hundred."

Hiram scratched his nose, "I guess the price of revolutionaries has just gone down."

"I'm going back!" Stanly said starting for his cell.

"Stanly," Hiram called after him.

Stanly suddenly stopped in mid-stride and stared at the lone figure in the cell before him.

"Larry," he said softly, "Larry Holbrook."

The figure looked up from the cot he was sitting on. "Do I know you?"

"We went to high school together."

The figure took a closer look. "Stan?"

"I saw you in the game last night, Larry," Stanly said.

Larry smiled a dazed smile, "Did we win?"

Stanly looked at him in bewilderment, "Don't you know?"

"Hell, I was so high last night, half the time I wasn't even sure which team I was playing on. Man, you should have seen it. After the game there were cops everywhere. We were in some chick's apartment, I just got the joint, and pow! they were everywhere."

Larry shook his head in disgust, "It's my own fault. I never should have smoked that joint at that chick's place. I was told this was going to happen some day. If you're going to smoke, do it on campus, it's the safest place. They never bust you on campus. But once you leave, pow! they're everywhere, they bust you just like that."

"Is there anything I can do?" Stanly asked.

"No. Coach will be here in a bit and bail me out. Coach can take care of anything. You know, Coach even buys my dope for me. It's all legal, of course," Larry continued. "You see, after every game we win the school buys us a steak dinner. Now steak dinners usually run around seven or eight bucks, so Coach offers us the dinner or five dollars in cash; we take the cash, Coach pockets the extra, we buy dope with our cut, and everyone is happy."

Larry smiled happily.

Stanly shut his eyes for a moment, then opened them, turned around and left without a word.

Outside the police station Hiram caught up with Stanly.

"I've got something for you," Hiram said.

"What?"

"I know you don't read papers, but I thought you might like to see this. I picked it up on the way over."

Hiram unfolded the newspaper he had with him and exhibited the bold headline to Stanly.

"Midwestern student arrested for inciting riot," Stanly read aloud and without emotion.

"There's a complete story of your brave stand against the campus pigs in here. According to this, and I quote, 'Stanly Allen, Midwestern's newest campus hero, has dared to take a stand against apathy and show that he gives a damn and will fight for what he believes in — even go to jail for his beliefs."

Hiram smiled at Stanly, "At this moment you're probably the greatest thing since Disneyland or pot. You're a hero."

Stanly shook his head.

"Something wrong?"

"All I did was stay standing," Stanly said, "I don't want to be a hero. All I want to be is an — "

"Artist," Hiram finished, "Let's go home."

Stanly lifted the phone off the hook, dialed three digits and then slammed the receiver back in its cradle.

"Calling someone, Stan?" Hiram asked.

"No."

The door unexpectedly broke open pinning Stanly against the wall.

"I think I got a girl pregnant!" Spike shouted, terror rising in his voice.

"Congratulations! And it's only four o'clock in the afternoon," Hiram said calmly, "What's wrong with you? Usually you don't bust in here till two o'clock in the morning with maniacal jibberings."

"I think I got a girl pregnant!" Spike screamed again.

"What do you mean?" Stanly asked as he tried to calm the overgrown leprechaun.

"I think I got a girl pregnant!" Spike continued to shout.

"You've said that already," Hiram said. "What do you mean you think you got her pregnant?"

"It wasn't my fault. She told me she was on the pill and when we got through, she said she wasn't."

"You better talk to Shelly." Hiram frowned. "He knows about things like this."

Spike scurried off toward Shelly's room and began pounding on the door and shouting, "I think I got a girl pregnant! I think I got a girl pregnant!"

Shelly opened the door.

"I'll bet you had a *ball*," Shelly said blankly.

"I think I got a girl pregnant!" Spike continued to scream.

"What's the matter with him?" Shelly asked.

"He thinks he got a girl pregnant," Hiram said.

"Tell him about it," Stanly told Spike.

Spike quickly related his tale to Shelly and then glanced hopefully at him for advice and guidance.

Shelly was quiet for a moment and then said, "What did you do with her when you were through?"

"I had her take a bath."

"Good," Shelly said. "That was the right thing to do."

"Then I carried her to her room."

"You carried her!" Hiram interjected.

"She has a hard time walking without her crutches."

"Crutches?" Stanly asked.

"You screwed a cripple!" Hiram burst into laughter.

"She's not a cripple! She just had a skiing accident and has a cast on her leg."

"You screwed a cripple," Hiram mused.

"Cast?" Stanly asked.

Spike turned back toward Shelly. "You don't think she's pregnant do you?"

"No, Spike," Shelly said, "you did the right thing with the bath. She won't get pregnant."

A look of ecstasy crossed Spike's pudgy little face as he started to scamper off down the hall.

"Have you ever seen any of the girls that Spike has got?"

"No," Stanly replied to Hiram's query.

"Ugly. Man, they're the ugliest. You know, I once wondered what people like Spike were put on this world for, and tonight I finally figured it out."

"What?" Shelly asked.

"Spike was put here to screw all the ugly women in the world. That's his sole purpose for being. Just look at all the ugly girls around here. You guys wouldn't touch them. I wouldn't. So what have they got?"

"Spike," Shelly said.

"That's right," Hiram continued, "Spike was put on this earth to screw all the ugly women. Give them something to remember in their old age. An affair!"

"Something they can tell their grandchildren about," Shelly added.

"I don't think they'd tell their grandchildren," Stanly said.

Hiram looked at Shelly, "You think he got that girl pregnant today?"

A slight smile spread across Shelly's features. "Probably," he said.

Spike came scampering back into sight. "Shelly!" he yelled, "Shelly, I just told her that she wasn't pregnant, and she said she was, and that she wants to marry me! Are you sure she isn't pregnant? Are you sure?"

"I'm sure," Shelly said without expression. "Who are you going to believe? Her or me? And, if I'm wrong I can always hypnotize her into thinking she's not."

"Can you really do that?" Spike asked hopefully.

"No," Shelly laughed, "I was just kidding. But I could hypnotize you into believing you didn't do it."

"You can hypnotize people?" Hiram asked incredulously.

"Sure," Shelly said.

"How do you do it?" Stanly asked.

"I talk to you," Shelly replied. "Hypnotism is just a matter of getting you to go to sleep. When you're awake your conscious controls your activity, but when you sleep your subconscious takes over. You have dreams. I just control your dreams, and make them real instead of mental illusions, that's all."

"Do it to me," Hiram said.

"All I need is someplace where there is complete silence," Shelly said.

"I don't want to be hypnotized!" Spike stated adamantly.

"Well I do," Hiram said. "Can you hypnotize me now?"

"Sure," Shelly answered. "Just find me a place that's quiet."

At that instant Far Out's stereo blurted out an explosion of music which reverberated down the entire length of the dorm hall.

Chapter V

"Shut off that goddamned music, Far Out!" Hiram yelled. The music ended as suddenly as it had begun.

"We can use our room," Hiram said.

"Lay down on the bed and take your shoes off," Shelly instructed when they were all inside. Hiram did as he was requested. "Now," Shelly continued, "this is going to take about half an hour. You guys can stay and watch if you want but I have to have complete silence."

Spike stood up, his incident with the girl already gone from his little mind. "I'll go make sure Far Out doesn't play his music."

"I'll stay," Stanly said sitting down on the floor.

"All right," Shelly said, "but be quiet. Now Hiram, I want you just to relax, and concentrate on my voice. . . ."

Twenty minutes later, Hiram opened the door to the room and tip-toed outside into the hall. Spike and Far Out were both waiting there.

"What happened?" Spike asked.

Hiram put a finger to his lips, "We were about half way through and it wasn't having any effect on me. Then Shelly saw Stanly lying on the floor sound asleep. He's just putting him into a deeper trance now."

Suddenly the door opened again and Shelly and Stanly walked out.

"Go into the lounge," Shelly told everyone.

"Is he under?" Spike asked.

"Did it work?" Far Out added.

Shelly shrugged his shoulders. "Go into the lounge," he repeated.

Everyone shifted toward the lounge, however, during the entire trip from the hall, around the corner, and into the lounge their eyes constantly darted back and forth between Shelly and Stanly.

"Have a seat," Shelly said when they had arrived at their destination. When everyone had, Shelly looked at Stanly and said, "Stan."

Stanly looked up, Shelly clapped his hands twice and Stanly toppled off of his chair sound asleep.

"What happened?" Spike asked in amazement.

"He's under," Shelly said simply.

"Far fucking out!" Far Out said.

"What do you do now?" Hiram asked.

"Now you can do anything with him you like."

"Do something," Spike said.

"Far fucking out!" Far Out repeated.

Shelly bent down toward Stanly's ear. "Stan," he said, "You are still in the deepest sleep you have ever been in. But when I count to three and snap my fingers you will wake up and remember nothing. However, when you hear Hiram say the word beer, you will have to go to the bathroom. And when I clap my hands twice you will fall back into the deepest sleep you have ever been in."

Shelly counted to three and snapped his fingers. Stanly's eyelids fluttered for a minute and then opened wide.

"What happened?" Stanly asked.

"Nothing," Shelly said, "I tried to put you under but I couldn't do it. Do you want a beer?"

"No," Stanly said, "I don't drink."

"Have a beer," Spike said.

Stanly looked at him blankly for a moment, "No, I don't drink."

"Stan," Hiram said.

"What?"

"B-E-E-R spells beer," Hiram smiled.

Suddenly Stanly's face contorted in bewilderment and he rushed out of the lounge as Spike and Far Out fell to the floor in uncontrolled rages of hysterical laughter.

"You see," Shelly explained, "because of the way the suggestion was worded, he responds only when Hiram says beer."

A few seconds later Stanly reappeared.

"Where did you go, Stanly?" Shelly asked.

Stanly shook his head. "I don't know. For some reason I just all of a sudden — I just — I . . . "

"Had to piss?" Spike added.

"Yeah."

"Maybe you need a beer, Stan," Hiram said.

A pained expression came over Stanly as he rushed from the room again.

"Far fucking out!" Far Out screamed between bursts of laughter.

Stanly struggled out of the men's room bedraggled and confused.

"What's going on?" he asked as they gathered about him.

"Beer!" Hiram said.

Without a word, Stanly turned and fled back into the bathroom.

"That's wild," Hiram said, "What else can you do with him?"

Stanly stepped out of the bathroom and Shelly clapped his hands twice.

"Catch him," Shelly shouted as Stanly collapsed back into sleep.

Spike grabbed Stanly and gently lowered him to the floor. Shelly leaned over Stanly, "The word beer will no longer affect you," he said. "But when I count to three and snap my fingers you will wake up, and you will be a circus clown entertaining the poor little orphans that are standing around you. When I clap my hands twice you will fall back into the deepest sleep you have ever been in; one, two, three." Shelly snapped his fingers. Stanly gave a jerk, opened his eyes and then stood up, a great half-assed grin working its way about his mouth.

"Hello, kiddies," Stanly said in a strange voice that was his, yet wasn't his. He then caught sight of his reflection in the window. "Oh," he said touching his face, "I'm not in make-up or costume yet."

"We don't care," Shelly said, "just give us a show."

"Yeah," Spike commented as he lit one of his cigars, "give us a show."

"Oh," Stanly said in a hurt voice, "You shouldn't be smoking at your age. It's bad for you. Now be a good little boy and give your friend Uncle Bebo that nasty old cigar."

Stanly extended his hand for the cigar.

"Far fucking out!" Far Out said with enthusiasm.

Uncle Bebo whirled around, "You should not say things like that. Where did a little boy like you learn such bad words?" He turned back to Spike, "Now please give Uncle Bebo the cigar."

Spike extended his middle finger at Uncle Bebo.

"You poor little thing," Stanly said, "I understand how hard it must be for you. Not having any parents to look after you or anything. But you 'mustn't smoke, you simply mustn't."

Spike blew smoke in Uncle Bebo's face.

"Is 'mustn't' a real word?" Hiram asked.

"Do a trick for us, Uncle Bebo," Shelly said.

"Yeah, do a trick, trick," Spike said.

"All right," Stanly consented, "but first you must give me that smelly old cigar."

Stanly reached over and took the cigar out of Spike's mouth.

"Hey!" Spike yelled, "give me back that cigar, dammit!"

"It's bad for you," Uncle Bebo explained.

"Come on," Hiram said, "show us a trick, Uncle Bebo."

"All right," Stanly agreed, "What would you like me to do?"

"Eat the cigar," Spike said disgustedly.

"Oh no," smiled Uncle Bebo, "that wouldn't be fun at all."

"Eat it or I'll cry," Spike threatened.

"But I – "

Spike suddenly sprawled out on the floor, kicking and screaming, "Eat it or I'll cry!"

"Little boy don't," Stanly begged, "Little boy don't! Don't! Please don't! All right, I'll eat it. I'll eat it, just don't cry. Look! Look! I'm eating it, I'm eating it," Stanly choked as he stuffed the tobacco into his mouth.

His face turned an off-green color as he swallowed the mess, but he managed a brave smile and said, "There, wasn't that a good trick?"

"No," Hiram said to Spike, "that was a stupid trick. I didn't like it at all."

"Not only that," Spike put in, completely unperturbed, "it was one of my best cigars. I want my money back. You're not a good clown at all."

Stanly went down on his knees, "I'm sorry," he said, "I'm sorry. I tried. I tried." Tears began to form in his eyes, "I'm sorry. You poor little orphans. I tried. I tried so hard to be a good clown," he sobbed as he broke down in a flood of tears.

"You better bring him out of it!" Hiram said.

Shelly clapped his hands twice and Stanly rolled over on his side sound asleep.

"Will he remember any of this?" Hiram asked.

"Not a bit," Shelly replied, "It will be just as if he has lost an hour's time and gained the equivalent of eight hours sleep. He'll probably be awake all night once I bring him out of it."

"You going to do anything more with him, it's almost time for supper," Hiram said.

"One more," Spike begged, "Do one more."

"Okay," Shelly agreed, "There is something I want to try anyway." Shelly crossed to where Stanly was sleeping peacefully on the floor and bent down. "Stanly," Shelly said, "you are no longer a clown. You are John Wayne. When I count to three and snap my fingers you will no longer be Stanly Allen or a circus clown, you will be John Wayne. One, two, three!"

Shelly snapped his fingers and Stanly opened his eyes, looked around, and then climbed to his feet saying "Howdy, boys!"

"How do you do, Mr. Wayne?" Shelly said.

"Duke," Stanly said with a wistful smile, "just call me Duke."

"Far fucking out," Far Out uttered.

"How's the movie business going?" Hiram asked.

"Fine," Stanly said, "just fine. Of course, every now and then we get a few commie pinko draft dodgers working on the set, trying to undermine this great nation of ours. THE UNITED STATES OF AMERICA," he said with a tear in his eye and his right hand over his heart, "but we take care of them in our way," he continued, drawing an imaginary gun from an imaginary holster at his hip. "God bless America," he said solemnly.

"Can I have your autograph, Mr. Wayne," Far Out asked,

sticking a pencil and paper into Stanly's hands.

"Certainly," Stanly said, "and just make it Duke, son."

He handed the paper back to Far Out.

"Best wishes from John 'Duke' Wayne." Far Out read aloud, "Far fucking out."

"Shelly stepped up beside Stanly, "Duke?"

"Yeah, son?"

"We've got a friend here that says he knows you real well. His name is Stanly Allen."

"Stanly Allen," Stanly repeated slowly.

"Yeah. Stanly Allen. He says you two are real good friends."

"Stanly Allen," Stanly said again, "Stanly Allen. Hell, yes! Close! Why we're just like two peas in a pod we're so close. Know him? Like I know myself — maybe better."

Shelly smiled and started to clap his hands twice.

"Hold it!" Hiram said grabbing his arm, "What are you going to do?"

"I'm going to bring him out of it," Shelly said, "I just wondered what would happen if I gave him another identity and then told him about himself. Now I know, so I thought I'd bring him out of the trance."

"Wait," Hiram said, "I want to do something."

"Duke," he said addressing Stanly.

"Yeah?"

"You say you and Stanly are friends?"

"Hell, yeah."

"Well, Stanly was about to make a phone call this afternoon, but never completed it; do you know who he was calling?"

"Of course," Stanly said, and then a troubled expression crossed his features. "You know," he said, "that little feller's got troubles."

"What kind of troubles?" Hiram asked.

"Gal trouble," Stanly said confidentially.

"Yeah?"

"Yessirree. He's got an ache in his heart fer this purty little filly."

"Was he calling her to ask for a date?"

"Yeah. But he'll never do it. He can't even get past the first three digits."

A mischievous gleam came to Hiram's eyes. "Maybe you can help him, Duke."

"Me? How can I help the little pardner?"

"Why don't you call the girl, tell her you are Stanly, and make the date for him."

"Now that's a right smart idea." Stanly smiled, "Hell, why didn't I think of that. I'll do it for him."

Stanly marched into his room, picked up the phone and began to dial as everyone crowded inside to listen.

"Hello," Stanly said, "this is Duke — "

"Stanly Allen!" Hiram hissed.

"I mean this is Stanly Allen, ma'am — and, well you see, ma'am, I was thinking that I'd be right powerful honored if you'd do the honor of accompanying Stanly — I mean me, to the homecoming. . .well, thankee kindly, ma'am. . .yes, ma'am. . .I'll see you then ma'am. . .good night, ma'am."

Stanly hung the phone up and gave a wild smile as everyone else waited expectantly.

"Stanly sure is going to be happy to find out what I done fer him," Stanly said.

"He sure is." Hiram laughed, "I'll be damned. Stanly got a date because of John Wayne. This is crazy."

Stanly just stood there beaming.

"What's her name? The girl you got Stanly a date with?" Hiram asked.

"Tracy Williams," Stanly said with a twinkle in his eye.

Complete and total silence encompassed the entire room.

"What did you say?" Hiram finally was able to ask after he had caught his breath.

"Tracy Williams," Stanly smiled.

Frantic and pained glances were quickly exchanged among the other members in the room.

"Oh my God," Spike gasped.

"What have we done?" Hiram asked.

"Gunther will kill him," Far Out stated.

"We just put Stan's head in a noose, and Gunther's going to be the one to pull the rope," Shelly said.

Stanly simply stood there smiling his John Wayne smile. Hiram grabbed him by the shoulders and began to shake him.

"You've got to call her back! Tell her it was a mistake! Tell her it was a joke! Tell her anything! But tell her you don't have a date with her, you're not taking her to homecoming, understand!"

"Of course," Stanly said, "I'm not taking her. Stanly is."

"You ass!" Hiram shouted, "Call her back and tell her you're — Stanly's not taking her to homecoming!"

"I can't do that," Stanly said.

"Why not!"

"Cause Stan wants to take her to homecoming."

"So what?"

"It's the American way," Stanly said placing his hand over his heart, "God bless America."

"My God! You ass! You ass!" Hiram screamed at him.

"That's purty stiff talk, boy," Stanly said, "better watch it or you might get shot right where you stand."

"Shelly!" Hiram gasped in desperation, "You better bring him out of this so we can talk some sense into him."

Shelly nodded his head and clapped his hands twice.

Stanly just stood there as straight and tall as John Wayne, smiling from ear to ear.

"What happened?" Hiram asked.

"I don't know," Shelly said and clapped his hands again.

Stanly continued to smile.

"What's the matter?" Hiram asked as the panic began to rise inside him.

"I don't know," Shelly repeated.

"I don't think you told him to fall asleep when you clapped your hands, the last time you were talking to him," Far Out said.

"What are you going to do?" Hiram said becoming more and more frantic.

"I don't know!" Shelly answered, climbing onto Hiram's wave of frustration. "I don't know. I've never had anything like this happen before."

Chapter VI

"He's not going to be this way forever is he?" Spike asked.

Shelly glanced at Stanly and shook his head. "No, at the most it will wear off within eight hours."

"Well what are we going to do with him in the meantime?" Hiram asked.

Shelly shrugged his shoulders.

"I'm getting hungry," Spike said.

"Same here," came Far Out's voice.

Hiram looked at Stanly who was busily practicing with his imaginary pistol, and then at Shelly, "Maybe we should take him down to dinner. Can he eat?"

"He can do anything John Wayne can."

"Let's eat," Spike prompted.

"I don't think it would hurt anything," Shelly said, "and if we don't, he's not going to have anything to eat all night."

"Duke," Hiram called, "would you like something to eat?"

"Whatever suits you just tickles me plumb to death," Stanly drawled.

"Didn't I hear that line in an old Henry Fonda movie the other night?" Hiram asked no one in particular.

"You don't think he's turning into Henry Fonda, do you?" Far Out gasped.

"No," Shelly said, "It doesn't work that way. He will be John Wayne until he falls asleep again and wakes up out of the trance."

"You mean," Hiram started, "all we have to do to bring him out of this is to get him back to sleep and then wake him up?"

"That should work," Shelly said.

"And if it doesn't?"

"He's no worse off than before."

"Let's get him drunk," Spike said, "that should get him sleepy. It always does for me."

A quick exchange of glances and nods and it was affirmed.

"But Stan doesn't drink," Hiram said.

"No," Shelly said, "But John Wayne does. First we'll go eat, then we'll go get drunk."

"Yeah," Spike added merrily.

"Duke," Shelly said walking up to Stanly, "would you care to join us in a drink after supper?"

"I'd be mighty pleased. In fact, I'm buying."

"We couldn't let you do that, Duke."

"Sure we could!" Spike ejaculated.

"If you don't, I ain't going," Stanly said.

"All right," Shelly consented, "let's go eat."

Far Out pushed the button for the elevator and they had their usual fifteen minute wait before it arrived. While the others were waiting Spike made a quick dash to the bathroom in an effort to make as much room as possible for his up and coming meal.

"I heard a joke," Hiram said as Spike trotted off. Hiram

was the official champion of the sixth floor for the worst jokes ever told. "Well you see, this patient went to see his doctor, and after the doctor examined him he said, 'God, are you sick. Wait here while I write you out a prescription, so he reached into his pocket for a pen but pulled out a rectal thermometer instead. He put it down, reached into his pocket again, and pulled out another rectal thermometer. He did this four more times, and each time the result was the same – a rectal thermometer. 'Shit!' the doctor said, 'some asshole's got my pen.' "

Spike came jogging around the corner just as the chortling was subsiding. The light above the elevator turned red and the doors slowly spread open.

"What's so funny?" Spike asked.

"I'll tell you at dinner," Shelly said as they all piled into the little box for the trip down.

There were six floors from whence they began their journey and the bottom, and the elevator stopped at every floor with a minimum of three passengers loading on board at each stop. So by the time the elevator finally came to rest it more closely resembled a full box of unsharpened pencils.

During the ride down some poor unfortunate girl had been defenselessly crushed up against Stanly because of the bulk of the elevator's population.

"Mighty sorry about the inconvenience, ma'am," Stanly said to her when the elevator stopped and people began squeezing out, "I sure wish I could make it up to you. I know," he said tipping his invisible cowboy hat, "let me take ya to this here homecoming shindig. I hear it's going to be a real rompin' stompin' hoedown!"

"Stan!" Hiram yelled at him.

The girl first gave Stanly a quizzical once-over and then turned to Hiram. "Is he drunk?"

"No," Hiram explained. "He's John Wayne."

"You're crazy," she said, "You're both crazy!" she

emphasized and scurried out of the elevator as quickly as she could.

"Does this mean, 'no,' ma'am?" Stanly called after her.

"I think it means, 'no,' Duke," Hiram said as they pried their bodies from the elevator walls and hurried toward the cafeteria for their usual quarter hour wait in line before they could eat.

Spike and Shelly ended up near the very end of the line.

"What was so funny upstairs?" Spike asked.

Shelly quickly told the joke and finished it just as they reached the food. They both filled up their trays and headed for the table where the others were already seated.

"That was a good joke. Has everyone else heard it?" Spike asked.

"Everyone except Hiram," Shelly said with a straight face.

"He hasn't heard it?" Spike asked as hopes of becoming the champion worst jokester of the 6th floor danced in his warped little mind.

"No."

"Hey, Hiram," Spike said as they reached the table and set their trays down, "I've got a joke for you."

"You've got a joke for me?"

"Yeah. Now stop me if you've heard it, okay?"

"Okay."

"You see this patient went into his doctor's office, and the doctor gave him a quick check up. 'Oh my,' the doctor said. 'You're really in bad shape, here let me write you a prescription.' So the doctor reached into his pocket where he kept his pen, but pulled out a rectal thermometer. He looked at it, then put it down and reached in his pocket again. Again he pulled out a rectal thermometer. He did this three more times and each time he pulled out a rectal thermometer. 'Shit' the doctor said — "

"Wait," Hiram said breaking in, "I've heard it."

"What?"

"I've heard it," Hiram repeated.

"All right smart ass," Spike demanded, "then what's the punchline?"

"Spike de Camp's got it," Hiram said without expression. Spike heard nothing except the wrong punchline.

"No!" he shouted in joy as a look of triumph transplanted his elf-like features. "The punchline is, 'some asshole's got my pen!' "

"That's what I said," Hiram said, again without any expression.

Ten full seconds passed, while everyone around him burst into laughter, before Spike realized what had just happened.

"You fuckhead!" he shouted grabbing a handful of jello and throwing it at Hiram. Fortunately for Hiram the jello missed him. Unfortunately for Spike, it hit Stanly.

"No one hits the Duke with jello," Stanly said picking up his tray and dumping the contents on Spike.

"You goddamned son-of-a-bitch!" Spike shouted as he picked up his own tray and returned the compliment.

Fragments from both trays made their way to other tables nearby with the result of these victims grabbing their food and splattering other innocent victims. In a matter of moments, the entire cafeteria was a blood-thirsty melee of flying food and curses.

After ten minutes a siren wailed in the distance. Suddenly the doors burst open and ten uniformed policemen entered.

"Campus Police!" Officer Rice shouted above the din, "Everyone break it up!"

Instantly, everyone dived for a seat. Everyone that is except Stanly who remained standing in the center of the room, war-splattered with remnants of what once was food.

Officer Rice nudged his partner, "That one standing must be their leader. We'll talk to him first. Damned hippies! C'mon, let's get this over with."

"I'm Officer Rice, head of campus riot control," he said to Stanly as he flipped his wallet out in front of him, "here is my badge and these are my cred — wait a minute," he said noticing Stanly for the first time. "Don't I know you?"

"Ever been to Hollywood?" Stanly replied.

"No, no — you're the one at the demonstration. Allen, Stanly Allen!"

" 'Fraid you got me confused with a friend of mine," Stanly said. "My names's Wayne — Mr. Wayne to you!"

Officer Rice was at the point of handcuffing Stanly for the second time that day when the head resident of the dorm intervened.

"Thank you for your help, Officer," he said. "We can handle it from here."

He turned to Stanly, "I want you here tonight at eight o'clock sharp to report your conduct to the Board of Concern, understand?"

"He'll be here," Hiram assured the head resident.

"We'll make sure he is," Shelly chimed in, "C'mon, Stan — Duke, let's get out of here before you get in any more trouble."

"I think we ought to run him in," Rice stated as the five silently crept out of the cafeteria.

"It will be all right," the Head Resident said, "the Board will take care of him; they'll probably stick him on probation."

"Probation!" Rice ejaculated. "You oughta stick him to the wall, get rid of punks like that completely! Expel him!"

"That's up to the Board. He's their problem now."

"Let's go," Rice said to his men. They left, leaving the cooks to stare in disbelief at the mess they had to clean up.

Outside Spike grabbed Stanly's arm, "That was really great, Duke, I sure enjoyed that fight," he said happily.

Stanly smiled as Hiram grabbed his other arm, "Yeah, that was just great, except you'll probably get expelled for it; put on probation at the very least."

"That's all right," Stanly smiled. "I'll just go back to Hollywood and make a few pictures if they do."

"Oh my God," Hiram uttered, "I need a beer. Now!"

"Don't you want to change first?" Shelly asked.

"No," Hiram stated, "the sooner we get yo-yo here back to normal the better. C'mon."

Dark was just beginning to settle in for the night when they arrived at the local 3.2 place off campus.

"Bring us a couple of pitchers of beer," Shelly instructed the waitress.

"I got to go to the bathroom," Spike uttered, rising and rushing for his destination in order to clear his system for bigger and better things to come.

By the time he returned the beer was just being served.

"You should see what I just saw," he said extending his mug for a helping.

"What?" Far Out asked.

"These two guys were holding this other guy up between them, because the guy in the middle was too drunk to stand up and take a piss by himself."

"Far fucking out," Far Out said.

"That's not the good part," Spike said.

"There's more?"

"Yeah. What he was peeing on was his contact lens."

"That's terrible."

"And one of the guys that was holding him up," Spike continued, "kept saying 'hit it again, Harold. I'll buy you another beer if you can hit it again!' "

Spike drained his mug and smiled contentedly as he poured himself another mugful.

"How do you feel?" Shelly asked as he poured another beer for himself and Stanly.

"Fine. Never felt better in my life."

"You don't feel sleepy?"

"Not a bit," Stanly grinned.

Spike was by this time consuming his fifth glass of beer. This was because Spike did not drink beer like normal people.

Normal people come up for air every now and then, Spike never did until he had finished everything off. It was his theory that beer should not be drunk slowly, but that each mug should be chugged.

Spike's little pig eyes, glued inside his elfish mask, turned a deep rich red. He swayed back and forth on his chair as he began refilling his cup. Then he spotted a waitress standing beneath a black light, her white uniform glowing a bright purple in the surrounding darkness.

"You look just like an angel under that light!" Spike yelled across the room at her.

"Shut up, Spike!" Hiram yelled at him.

"Bring me another pitcher!" Spike yelled at the world.

As the waitress responded to his call and set another brimming pitcher of beer before him, Spike gallantly raised his empty mug in a salute of chivalry to her charming beauty. But for all the nobility of intention, somehow, when combined with his half-assed grin and blood-shot drunk eyes, the scene was completely ludicrous and distinctly out of place.

"You know," Hiram whispered to Shelly, "Spike reminds me of my father. I have a feeling that's the same way my old man used to put the make on girls. Twenty or thirty years ago Spike would have been great. But today. . . "

"Yeah," Shelly answered, "I know what you mean. I used to wonder how he got so many lays; especially with his looks and those lines. But all you have to do is look at the girls he gets. They're the kind that's never going to get it. He knows it, and they know it. So he gives them something to remember in their old age and they give him something to control his horniness for a few hours. But look at him now trying to put the make on her. You know that there's no way, no chance in the world, and all he's going to do is make an ass of himself."

Spike grabbed the waitress' hand.

"Captain Horny strikes again!" Hiram whispered harshly.

"Gee, that's a beautiful ring you've got," Spike said slipping a cracker-jack's toy off her finger and trying to focus on it.

"Thank you," she said trying to get it back.

"Let me put it back on for you," he said shoving it down her middle finger. Her remaining fingers clutched together leaving the one remaining finger protruding straight up in front of Spike's face.

"That's so lovely," he said.

"Isn't it," she agreed with him, leaving the finger to linger in front of his face for a few more seconds.

"Let's dance," Spike said.

"I'm on duty."

"C'mon," he pleaded.

She turned and walked off without another word.

"You sure have nice shoes," Spike called after her, raising his mug in a farewell salute.

"You stupid ass," Shelly said.

Spike smiled drunkenly, wavered for a moment, then fell off his chair, landing spread-eagle on the floor, sound asleep.

"What do you think we ought to do with him?" Far Out asked.

"Leave him there," Hiram said. "With any luck and this size crowd nobody will notice him."

"Are you kidding?" Far Out questioned.

"It sounds like a good idea to me," Shelly said, "That way we won't have to carry him home. Let's finish our beer and go. When he wakes up he can find his way home. . .maybe."

They downed the remaining beverage and stumbled over the top of Spike's body, and out into the street.

"You feel sleepy, Duke?" Hiram asked.

"Nope," Stanly replied, "never felt better in my life."

"Maybe we should take him back to the dorm and push him out one of the windows," Shelly said.

"Yeah," Hiram agreed. "A fall from the sixth floor ought to put him to sleep."

"Hey," Far Out slurred, "if you're going to push him out the window, why don't we give Spike's new commando parachute a trial run."

Hiram nodded his head, "That's a good idea. It'll be like killing two birds with one stone — so to speak."

Shelly shook his head negatively, "That's a bad idea. A jump from the sixth floor will only rip the chute to pieces. We better push him from the twelfth floor. It will be safer that way."

"You're right," Hiram consented as he checked his watch. "It's seven thirty now. If we hurry we can get back to the dorm, push Stan out of the twelfth floor window, wake him out of his trance once he hits the bottom, and get him to the Concern Board meeting before eight."

"Right," Shelly said as he grasped Stanly's right arm, while Hiram took his left.

"I've also got some firecrackers we could shoot off!" Far Out called after them.

Chapter VII

Stanly wavered back and forth on the window ledge of the twelfth floor as he tried to gain a secure balance. Strapped to his back was a drag chute, the kind used in slowing racing cars to a brakeable spead.

"I've got my firecrackers ready," Far Out said.

"You ready, Duke?" Hiram asked,

Stanly nodded his head and flashed his John Wayne smile.

"I don't think we should do this," Shelly said.

Hiram stared at him, "Why not?"

"We didn't ask Spike if we could use his chute."

"I don't think he'd mind," Far Out added.

"Besides, it's only a drag chute," Shelly continued, "not a real parachute."

"You think that might make a difference?"

"It might."

"Maybe we should use a dummy first."

"We've already got a first class dummy on the ledge, but maybe we should."

"Duke," Hiram said, "Climb back on in here for a second, we're gonna try another dummy first."

Stanly inched his way back inside as the others began stripping and stuffing their clothes inside each other to create a make-shift dummy. In a matter of seconds they had a fully clothed creation while they stood decked in nothing more than their jocky shorts and socks.

They hastily transferred the drag chute from Stanly's back to the dummy's, then placed the dummy on the window ledge.

"Can you make a siren noise?" Shelly asked Far Out.

Far Out opened his mouth and began a long low wail.

Hiram shoved the dummy off the ledge and yanked the rip cord. Far Out seeing the dummy begin its descent, carefully aimed a pop-bottle rocket at the figure and struck a match. A soft whiz and the rocket shot after the dummy, striking it in the head as it colorfully lit up the sky. The impact, however, caused the dummy to somersault, tipping upside down.

Face down the dummy plunged in its fall toward earth, followed by a barrage of fireworks, and Far Out's siren noises.

Watching the dummy's ungraceful descent, Shelly noticed that an ever increasing crowd was forming outside.

Suddenly from below a flashlight beam cut through the dimness illuminating the dummy.

"Oh my God!" the student assistant holding the flashlight screamed, "someone jumped out the window!"

Shelly grabbed hold of Far Out and shouted in his ear.

"We've got to get rid of those people!" he indicated, pointing at the ever enlarging mass.

Far Out smiled happily, aimed a handful of pop-bottle rockets at the center of the group and struck a match. Instantly people were scattering every which way in search of shelter from Far Out's gayly exploding missiles. Far Out chuckled jubilantly.

Amazingly, even through Far Out's attack, the student assistant with the flashlight had kept the beam staunchly directed on the dummy through its entire flight, and now as it hit the ground, head first with a sickening crunch, the light held its course.

"Oh, God!" the student assistant cried. "He's broken his neck! We've got to help him!"

The mob thronged toward the dummy.

"Keep the student asses away from the dummy!" Shelly commanded.

Far Out broke out his artillery and once again the crowd dispersed in search of a safe haven.

"We've got to get that dummy before anyone else," Shelly said as the effects of the alcohol began to wear off.

"We don't have any clothes on," Hiram mentioned.

"Stan's still got on all his clothes," Far Out stated, as he touched off another rocket.

"Looks like you're the one that's going to have to do it, Stan," Shelly said.

"You talking to me?" Stanly asked.

"Of course I'm talking to you," Shelly said, "who else would I be talking to?"

"Stanly," Stanly said.

"You're. . .Duke," Shelly realized, "Duke, this is a script from your next picture. One of your buddies has been shot down over Berlin, you've got to rush down stairs and get to him before the Nazis, we'll cover you from here. Ready? Lights, camera, action! Roll 'em!"

Without hesitation Stanly rushed down the twelve flights of stairs to the bottom as Far Out kept the fireworks flying fast and furious. In the distance there came a long low wail.

"Rotten Nazis!" Stanly yelled as he reached the last flight, "Watch it, 'cause Big Duke is coming through!"

Stanly made a desperate rush toward the dummy dodging invisible bullets and Far Out's very visible fireworks.

"God bless America!" Stanly shouted as he reached the dummy and scooped it up in his arms.

A spotlight unexpectedly burst forth upon Stanly and a megaphoned voice reverberated, "Hold it right there, son. Campus Police! You're under arrest."

Stanly felt himself being forcibly shaken. He opened his eyes and focused on his setting: a too familiar looking cell.

"Nice to see you again," David Williams said as Stanly glanced about in bewilderment.

"Where am I?"

"In jail," Williams replied.

Stanly grabbed his head, "What? How did I get here? What happened? What's going on?"

"They told us you attacked the entire Campus Police department shouting 'I'll get you Nazis.' Then when they overpowered you, you started yelling 'director, cut it and print it.' Then they said you just fell asleep right in their arms."

"You're really cool," Joe said.

"What happened?" Williams asked, "have a little too much to drink, or smoke?"

"No," Stanly said, "this doesn't make sense. I was in my room watching this friend of mine get hypnotized. And now I'm here. This doesn't make sense. This doesn't make any sense at all."

Stanly stopped his rambling and glanced up at Williams.

"Didn't your sister come for you?"

"Yeah," he said, "she came, but she said she wasn't going to bail us out this time. She said if we had to spend the night here maybe next time we'd be more careful about getting caught."

"You mean you and Joe are going to have to stay here all night with me?"

"No. She always says that, then two or three hours later she comes back and bails us out."

Stanly shook his head sadly, "I wish I knew what was going on."

A guard appeared at the front of the cell, "Come on, Allen," he said, "your bail's been paid."

Stanly held his head tightly, "I feel like I've been through all this once before," he said. "Who paid my bail this time?"

"You'll see," the guard said leading Stanly out of the cell.

"See you again sometime," Williams called impishly.

Stanly could only wave limply as he staggered down the isle.

"Why did you bail me out?" Stanly asked, "How did you even know I was in jail?"

Larry Holbrook stuck his hands deep in his pockets. "Coach took care of everything here for me, just like I said he would. Then he told me to go home and get a good night's sleep, Coach always says things like that, and that we would talk about it in the morning. So, I was heading back to the dorm when I saw you being arrested for tossing that dummy out the window. And I bailed you out because I like you, and I. . .I needed to talk to you, Stan," he said.

"Dummy?" Stanly asked, then thought better of it and decided maybe it would be best if he didn't ask. "You wanted to talk to me? About what?"

"Sheila."

"Sheila?"

"You know we've been dating since high school."

"I know," Stanly said, "now."

"Well she's been getting very uptight lately, I mean about my smoking dope and everything. And, well since we went to high school together, and she knows you and I know you, and – do you know what I'm trying to say?"

"Not at all."

"She won't go to homecoming with me. She won't even talk to me about it, and on a campus this size there are a lot of guys, and I don't want any one of those bastards touching

Sheila, and well — you don't have a date do you?"

"No," Stanly said slowly.

"Well, I want you to take Sheila to homecoming for me. To see that no one gets a chance to put a move in on her."

"What?"

"I mean we went to high school together and everything. I know I can trust you; since she won't go with me, I want you to take care of her for me until we can straighten out our differences."

"But — Stanly interposed, trying to recall if he had even seen Larry more than half a dozen times in all the years that they went to high school together.

"Is there someone else you were going to take?"

Stanly was silent for a minute and then shook his head. "No. I guess not. It never would have worked out anyway."

"Good, then you'll take her. And, Stan, if ever I can do the same for you, you just let me know."

"I don't know."

"This is important to me, Stan, she gives me a lot of shit, sure, but I love her, Stan. And I don't want to take a chance on losing her. You can understand that. Will you do it for me, please?"

"Stanly!" a voice cut through the night as two figures came rushing toward him.

"I thought we'd never find you," Hiram gushed out of breath.

"They told us at the police station that someone had already paid your bail," Shelly added.

"This is Larry Holbrook," Stanly said, "we went to high school together; he bailed me out."

"It's a good thing," Hiram commented, "I couldn't find anyone at the dorm to loan me any money to bail you out. They all think you're making this too regular a habit to to make it worth getting you out. Which I don't blame them, cause just as soon as you're out, you're working on a way to get back in."

"Speaking of getting in, how did — " Stanly began.

"I'm Shelly Richards," Shelly cut Stanly off in mid-sentence, introducing himself and Hiram to Larry Holbrook.

"Stan," Hiram said, "We've got to talk to you — privately."

"I was just leaving," Larry said, "You will do it for me, won't you, Stan?"

Stanly nodded his head slowly, as if he was giving his consent to walk cheerfully into the jaws of hell.

"Thanks, Stan. Good night, it was nice meeting you guys. See you later, Stan. And thanks again."

"Night," Shelly called after him, "And thank you for bailing Captain Klutz out for us."

"Stan," Hiram began as Larry disappeared into the night, "we've got to tell you something."

Stanly held up his hand, "First," he said quietly, "tell me how I got in jail."

"That's part of it," Shelly continued for Hiram, "You see, you went under when I was trying to hypnotize Hiram, so it's partly your fault too. Anyway, I made you John Wayne, and then when you tried to rescue a dummy we pushed out the window, the cops caught you, and thought you had pushed the dummy out the window. And since we didn't have any clothes on we couldn't come down and tell them we did it. Not that we would even if we did have clothes on, but that's neither here nor there, 'cause you thought the cops were Nazis in a movie you were making, so you attacked them. That's why you were put in jail. But that's not important."

"I didn't understand a word you said," Stanly protested, "and even if I had I wouldn't believe you. What do you mean that's not important?"

Hiram wrung his hands, "I'm not sure how to put this, but I think we just set you up to get rubbed out unless you act very quickly."

"What are you talking about?"

"Gunther's going to kill you."

"What?"

"When I made you John Wayne," Shelly explained, "you made a date with a girl for homecoming."

"What?"

"Yeah," Hiram bubbled, "Tracy Williams."

"What?"

"It's true. When you make a date, you don't mess around, you're about as subtle as a hair in a biscuit."

"I've got a date with Tracy Williams?"

"Yeah. That's why you've got to call her back right now, and break it."

"I've got a date with Tracy Williams for homecoming," Stanly said to himself. "What do you mean I've got to call her back and break it?"

"Didn't you hear what we said?" Hiram asked, "The girl you asked to homecoming was Tracy Williams. Gunther will kill you when he gets back from Nebraska if you don't."

"So?" Stanly said with a look of defiance shining in his eyes.

"What? Jesus, Stan. Sometimes you're frustrating as hell! What do you mean 'so'?"

"I can't help who I fall in love with," Stanly said slowly and deliberately, "I wish I could, but I can't!"

"What?" Hiram and Shelly asked in unison.

Chapter VIII

On any university campus, or in any maximum security prison, there is a grapevine through which news travels with a speed unrivaled by any press service in the world. How it works will probably remain one of the great mysteries of our time. Why it works, is because people are naturally curious about anything and everything which shouldn't concern them in the least. But, needless to say, work the grapevine does, and by Monday morning Midwestern University was a-buzz with the legend of its newest anti-hero, as he had now been designated: Stanly Allen demonstrating against the war; Stanly Allen leading a food fight in rebellion against the slop students were forced to eat; Stanly Allen igniting fireworks and ejecting dummies out of twelve story buildings in defiance of dormitory regulations; Stanly Allen waging war obstinately against the "pigs" in order to bring about a student ruled university.

But all these events, regardless of the true circumstances behind their happening, were reduced to the minutest of significance when compared to Stanly Allen's latest episode: Stanly Allen defying Mike Gunther and taking Tracy Williams to homecoming.

"You ass!" Hiram ejaculated, "My God! You dumb ass! What are you going to do when Gunther gets back from Nebraska and comes up to you and says, 'your name Allen?' "

"I'll very calmly look him in the eye and say, 'who me? No. My name is Burroughs. Hiram Burroughs. Allen is a tall thin guy with blond hair and black horn-rimmed glasses,' that's what I'll say."

"You bastard. You would too, wouldn't you?"

"Yes."

The door suddenly swung open and Spike, having recovered from his hangover, made his way back to the dorm, and learned of the events concerning Stanly and Saturday night, strutted in.

"Hey you hamburger," Spike said. "What would you do if Gunther showed up here today?"

"Get out of here, Spike," Hiram said.

Shelly slipped into the room behind Spike.

"Morning," he said, "Stan, what are you going to do when Gunther gets back from Nebraska?"

Stanly broke into hysterical laughter. When he was finally able to gain control of himself he gave a wane smile.

"I'll get lawyers," he said, "If he lays a hand on me, it will be the sorriest day of his life."

"I have a feeling," Hiram said, "that it will also be the sorriest day of your life."

Stanly continued to smile weakly.

"Yeah," he said softly.

"Hey, Stan," Hiram began, "I hate to bring this up, with all that's going on and everything, but your paper's due this Friday."

"My what?"

"Your term paper on canals."

"Oh."

"You goin' to do it?"

"No!"

"Homecoming's this Friday, too."

"Yeah?"

"You've still got time to break your date with Tracy."

"No!"

"Why not for chrissake!"

"Because I love her."

Hiram was speechless for a second, "Are you going to start that again? You don't even know her, you only met her once. How do you know you love her?"

"I know," Stanly said.

"You don't!" Hiram shouted.

"I do!" Stanly shouted back.

"All right," Hiram gave in. "Maybe you do. Maybe you love her. But so what? What are you going to do about Gunther? He's going to kill you when he gets back, and it seems awful stupid to die just because you love a girl. A girl that may not even love you."

"You don't know that she doesn't!"

"Yes, but you don't know that she does," Hiram returned, "And that's the whole point. You don't know what you're getting yourself into."

"I don't care."

Hiram shook his head, "Are you going to class today?"

"No."

"You dumb ass, you're flunking five classes and you're not going to class today!"

"I'm going to see Tracy."

"To tell her you can't take her?"

"No!" Stanly emphasized, "to make plans."

"What kind of plans – mass suicide?"

"About when I'll pick her up, not that it's any of your

business. Hand me that telephone book so I can get her address."

"She won't be home," Shelly said.

"What?"

"They're selecting the homecoming queen today. Since she's one of the candidates she'll be there."

"Where?"

Shelly tossed him a paper, "If you'd learn how to read a newspaper you'd know. See, right next to the picture of you being arrested by the police, it says the queen candidates will be at our multimillion dollar, soon to be obsolescent, football stadium at one o'clock, at which time the Queen shall be chosen. Isn't that amazing?"

Stanly read the article, then skimmed over the story about himself.

"The Concern Board sure was pissed off when you didn't show up at the meeting Saturday night," Hiram said, interrupting Stanly's reading.

"I know," Stanly said, "I got a letter from them this morning. They said I'm on probation for the rest of the quarter, and if I do anything else like Saturday night they're going to kick me out of school."

"You're really something, Stan," Hiram said, "You're the only person I know who is being threatened to get kicked out of college by the administration because of your grades, by the Concern Board because of your activities, and by Gunther because you're fooling around with his chick. Only if Gunther kicks you out of school it will be permanent in more ways than one."

Stanly crumpled up the newspaper in his hand, threw it in the waste basket, and quietly left the room.

Stanly made his way through the crowded football stadium. Then he saw Tracy sitting on a raised platform with the other queen candidates in the middle of the football field. As Stanly started toward her, firm fingers grasped his shoulder. Stanly spun around and stood facing Larry Holbrook.

"Hi, Stan," Larry said, "and thanks a lot."

"For what?"

"For getting Sheila and me back together. I told her you wanted to take her to homecoming, then when she found out you were going with Tracy Williams, she came running to me saying how inconsiderate some people can be about other people's feelings, not caring who they hurt, and that she didn't realize how lucky she was to have me until she met you, even though I do take a little dope now and then I would never do anything like that at least."

"What?" Stanly asked as Larry began pumping his hand vigorously up and down.

"Sheila's going to homecoming with me because you dropped her," Larry explained.

Stanly slapped his forehead with the palm of his free hand, "I'm sorry," Stanly apologized, "I forgot all about that."

"It worked out just perfect," Larry continued not even hearing Stanly, "I'll never be able to repay you for getting us back together again. Thanks, Stan."

"You're welcome," Stan said, not knowing what else to say.

"I want you and Tracy to come over to my place, before the dance Friday, for a few drinks," Larry grinned.

"I don't drink," Stanly started to say, but Larry cut him off, "See you then, and thanks again, Stan," he said as he disappeared into the crowd rejoining Sheila who waved at Stanly only out of courtesy (and because Larry had threatened to drop some mescaline if she didn't) before they both dissolved into nothingness.

Stanly turned and started for Tracy again when Shelly and Hiram appeared on either side of him.

"Stanly?" Hiram said.

"What?"

"You know I'm your friend, Stan. That's why I said those things to you back in the room."

"I know," Stanly said.

"And I feel responsible for you," Hiram said. "I mean after all if I hadn't made a date with Malcolm's sister, who is Tracy's best friend, I wouldn't have met Tracy and been able to introduce you to her."

"You don't have to feel responsible."

"I just don't want you to get hurt, Stan."

"I won't get hurt."

"I don't mean just physically."

"I won't get hurt," Stanly repeated.

"Stan," Shelly said.

"What?"

"Since you're dead set on going ahead with this, and getting yourself killed, I won't try and stop you. Anyway, I'm taking Jan to homecoming, and I just wondered if you and Tracy wanted to double with us, since you don't have a car we could use mine."

"Okay," Stanly said, "thank you, Shelly."

Shelly nodded.

"You going to see her now?" Hiram asked.

"Yes."

"Good luck, dumb ass," Hiram said with a shrug of his shoulders. "Have a good one."

Stanly made his way to the edge of the crowd just as the president of the student body raised a glimmering crown on a plush red velvet cushion for the audience to view.

"This year as in previous years, the homecoming queen has been selected by a popular vote of the student body, and your homecoming Queen for this year is," He paused very dramatically, breathing heavily into the microphone while walking slowly behind each girl until, "Miss Tracy Williams," he said in his imitation of Bert Parks as he placed the crown over her flowing blonde hair, and a kiss on her cheek.

A flood of flashbulbs exploded amongst the applause and cheers. People came gushing out of the stands to give their congratulations as Tracy said something inaudible into the microphone which was supposed to pass as her acceptance speech. Then she saw Stanly standing quietly at the edge of the crowd. She flittered down the stairs of the platform and threw her arms around his neck, weeping softly on his shoulder.

"I never expected anything like this would happen to me," she cried happily.

"I never expected anything like this would happen to *me*," Stanly said soberly.

"I want to talk to you," he said after an eternity, although talk was not exactly the uppermost thought in Stanly's mind as he stood holding Tracy Williams in his arms.

"And I need to talk to you, after this," she said as a half a million students clustered about them.

"Tracy!" Stanly shouted, but his words died out in the din as Tracy was carried away with the tide of bubbling people trying to shake her hand or kiss her, mainly the latter, and mainly male.

Half an hour later the last of the nescient mob was dispersing and Tracy came up beside Stanly who was sitting on the grass at the fifty yard line, trying to recall snappy lines from old Erroll Flynn films.

"I'm sorry about all this," she said.

Stanly leaped to his feet knocking over the fifty yard marker.

"You wanted to speak to me?" she asked taking his hand.

At her touch, Stanly's mind went blank.

"What?" he came back with his usual finesse.

"I asked if you wanted to talk to me?"

"About what?"

"I don't know."

"Oh yes." Stanly nodded. "About when you want me to pick you up and things."

"All right. But first I want to ask you something."

Stanly gazed at her blankly trying to think what Erroll Flynn would say.

"And I want you to tell me the truth."

Stanly nodded his head, since he couldn't think what Erroll Flynn would say in a similar situation.

"You didn't ask me to homecoming because you felt sorry for me, did you?"

Stanly felt the world spin and a kaleidoscope of colors flash past his glazed eyes. It was so ridiculous, so ludicrous. Here was a goddess asking a mortal a question like that.

"Sorry for you?" Stanly asked incredulously.

"Because I didn't have a date."

"Sorry for you?" Stanly said because he couldn't think of anything else to say. "No, no never," Stanly stammered, "Me? For you? Are you kidding?"

"Are you sure?"

"I've never been so sure of anything in my life. I — "

"We've got a busy week planned for you two," the president of the student body said coming up beside Stanly and shoving a schedule in his hands. "Parades, rallies, football games. It's going to be a fun-filled week. As queen you'll have to attend all such functions, and of course since Mr. Allen is your escort he should be with you."

"You know me?" Stanly asked.

The president cleared his throat and Stanly noticed a paper with the picture of his scene with the police on it, slung under his arm, "Only by reputation, Mr. Allen," he said, "only by reputation. Well good day, Tracy. Mr. Allen, don't forget the parade tomorrow. Check the schedule for the correct time and place, and for all the rest of the events you are expected to attend."

"My brother's told me a lot about you," Tracy said as the student body president wandered off to console the losers. "He says he really likes you."

"Do I know your brother?"

"He said he met you in. . .in jail," she blushed.

"In jail?"

"Saturday, after the demonstration you led."

"I didn't lead the — after the demonstration? Your brother's David Williams?"

"Yes, I thought you knew."

"I want to explain about that — about my getting arrested," Stanly began.

"You don't have to. I think it's the bravest thing I ever heard of."

"It wasn't my fault. All I did was stand — you do?"

"And if there were more people concerned about the welfare of others, like you, this would be a lot better world to live in."

Stanly stared at her in disbelief, "The bravest thing. . . "

Suddenly a car horn brought Stanly back to reality.

"That must be my brother," Tracy said, "I've got to go now."

Stanly followed her out to the parking lot, "When will I see you again?"

"Hi, Stan," David Williams said as he opened the car door for his sister. "It's nice to see you somewhere besides in jail."

"I'll see you tomorrow at the parade," Tracy said climbing into the car, "Check the schedule."

Stanly waved absent-mindedly as Williams floored the accelerator, showering the waving figure with dust and pebbles.

"How did it go, Stanly?" Hiram's voice came from behind.

Stanly turned around as Shelly and Hiram approached him.

"I always wondered what it would be like to be Errol Flynn," he said, "now I know."

"Errol Flynn?" Hiram asked, "who's Errol Flynn?"

CHAPTER IX

"Parades, rallys, football games. It's going to be a fun filled week," is what the student body president had said.

"Parades, rallys, football games! This is ridiculous," Stanly mumbled.

"It's a bunch of shit, all right," Hiram replied, "but then have you ever known any homecoming activities that weren't?"

"I haven't seen Tracy all week," Stanly grumbled.

"You've been with her everyday."

"Yeah, at the parades, the rallys, and the football games with fifteen million goggling chaperons. I'd like to see her alone. Just once at least."

"Why don't you see her at night?"

"She works at night."

"Where?"

"Some restaurant."

"Go to her work."

"I did."

"Well?"

"Her boss doesn't allow visitors while she is working."

"Go as a customer."

"I did."

"And?"

"I was given another waitress."

"Did you wait for her after work to take her home?"

"Yes. But I forgot my wallet, and since I had ordered three dollars and twelve cents worth of dinner, which I did not eat, they wouldn't let me leave until I called Shelly and had him bring me some money. By that time her brother had already come and picked her up."

"You're a regular ball of fire when it comes to romancing a girl, aren't you?"

"Leave me alone."

"I'm on your side, Stan. I think it's great that you're dating Tracy."

"You do?"

"But Gunther is still going to kill you when he gets back and finds out what you've been doing."

"I don't care. I love her."

"Does she know that?"

"I don't know."

"Have you even talked to her about it?"

"With fifteen million spectators?"

"It's Friday," Hiram said, shifting the flow of the conversation.

"So what?"

"Your term paper is due today."

"I don't care."

"You didn't do it, did you?"

"No. And since I'm not going to class anyway, it doesn't matter."

"You could get kicked out of college."

"I don't care about that either. It's not important anymore."

"What is important?"

"I don't know."

"Being an artist?"

"No — yes; it's important, but not like before."

"You're crazy — or sick, or maybe both."

"Maybe he's in love," Shelly said as he opened the door without knocking and sauntered in.

"Don't you ever knock?" Hiram asked, "and that's a bunch of bullshit! No one falls in love with a chick at first sight — not even Stanly Allen."

"Not even Stanly Allen," Shelly repeated as he tossed a magazine on Stanly's desk, "I almost forgot why I came over. Here's your mail, they stuck it in my box again. When do you want to leave tonight, Stan?"

"I don't care."

"Well, the dance starts at nine. I figure if we leave by six-thirty we can pick up Jan and Tracy, get something to eat, go to Holbrook's party, and then on to the dance."

"All right. You sure you don't want to come with us, Hiram?"

"Yeah, I'm sure. I have got some acquainting to get done with Malcolm's sister during that time. I'll meet you later at the dance."

"Okay," Shelly said, "see you at six thirty then, Stan."

At half past six that evening, "I'm leaving now," Hiram called as he opened the door.

"Hi," Shelly said coming in, "you going to get Malcolm's sister now?"

"Yeah," Hiram grasped Shelly by the arm and led him back out into the hall, "Shelly," he said, "you better keep an eye on Stanly tonight. He still thinks he's in love with Tracy, so there's no telling what he might do in his condition."

"I'll watch out for him," Shelly assured him.

"Well, see you at the dance then," Hiram said as he headed for the elevator.

"Stanly!" Shelly called going back into the room. "You about ready to go?"

Stanly stepped out of the bathroom resplendent in a dark navy blue, double breasted sport coat with silver buttons; white checkered pants, and sneakers.

"Sneakers?" Shelly asked in disbelief, "You're wearing sneakers to the dance?"

Stanly glanced down at his grass-stained tennis shoes. "I don't have anything else," he said.

"Maybe Far Out or Spike has an extra pair of dark shoes you can borrow," Shelly hoped, "we can check on our way out. You all ready to go?"

"I guess so," Stanly said, and then noticed the small white box Shelly had in his hand.

"What's that?"

"It's a corsage for Jan."

"A corsage!" Stanly panicked, "I forgot to get one for Tracy!"

"I hope she likes orchids," Shelly said calmly.

"Orchids?" Stanly repeated.

"I had a feeling you would fuck it up," Shelly explained, "so I got you a corsage for her when I picked up Jan's."

"Shelly, how can I ever thank you?"

"Just give me the eleven dollars and fifty cents you owe me for the flowers."

"Eleven dollars!"

"And fifty cents — you wanted me to get the best for her, didn't you?"

"Yeah, but eleven dollars and fifty cents?" Stanly said reaching for his billfold and removing the money and handing it to Shelly.

"Let's go see if we can find you some decent shoes," Shelly said handing Stanly the corsage and leading him next door to Far Out and Spike's room.

Shelly pounded on the door.

"Who is it?" came a suspicious voice.

"Far Out has been smoking grass again," Shelly smiled, "cause he never asks, 'who is it,' he always just shouts to come in."

Shelly started pounding and kicking at the door. "This is the police! Open this door you fucking hippies! This is a bust!"

The sound of bodies tripping over one another as paranoia and hysteria running rampant echoed through the fake wooden door into the hall. Shelly gave a slight chuckle at the pandemonium he had created.

"Far Out!" he called, "It's me, Shelly. I was just kidding, Far Out."

An endless silence came from within the room. Then the sound of metal scraping metal as the chain was removed from its socket. Slowly the door inched open to reveal two fuzzy eyes, red rimmed from fright and grass.

"Shelly?" asked a quivering voice.

"Yeah, Far Out," Shelly replied. "Now let me in. It was only a joke."

The door opened the rest of the way and Stanly and Shelly stepped into the room. Far Out quickly shut and bolted the door behind them.

"That wasn't funny," Far Out commented in a blurry voice.

It took a couple of seconds before Stanly and Shelly grew accustomed to the dim lighting of the room, and the bittersweet aroma of marijuana that wafted through the thin atmosphere.

In the corner, slumped over a plastic chair was Malcolm, at his feet, his sister was starting to light up another joint.

"I thought you had a date with Hiram," Shelly said to Malcolm's sister.

"Who?" she asked blankly.

"Hiram," Shelly repeated. "His roommate," he said indicating Stanly.

"Oh, yes," she smiled. "I forgot all about that."

"He just left to pick you up," Shelly explained.

"Really? How thoughtful." She took a deep drag on the weed, and then very slowly exhaled.

"Don't you think you ought to be there?"

Malcolm's sister sucked on the joint once again. She looked up hazily at Shelly and smiled a half-ass smile.

"Well?" Shelly asked.

She shrugged her shoulders, then very tenderly kicked her brother in the shins.

"Huh?" he started up out of the plastic chair.

"Maybe you better take me home, Malcolm."

"Aw, I was just beginning to enjoy myself," Malcolm complained.

Malcolm's sister very gently took his right hand in hers, then carefully began bending his fingers back at the joint, "Take me home now or I'll break your fucking fingers off you stupid bastard," she said softly.

Malcolm howled in pain as he wisely consented.

"What do you guys want?" Far Out asked as Malcolm and his sister exited from the room.

"Stanly needs some shoes."

"Far fucking out."

"Black dress shoes."

"I got a pair," Far Out said happily.

"Good, can we borrow them?"

"They're all full of piss."

"What?"

Far Out pointed toward his closet, stretched out in front of it, lying spread eagle and snoring contentedly was Spike.

"He came in here about an hour ago," Far Out explained, "as drunk as a dog's ass. He had three joints with us and then started shouting 'I gotta take a whiz,' so he did — in our closet.

Shelly didn't even have to check the closet to verify if the dark shoes had been one of the luckless objects to be sprayed, the stench was enough to assure him that nothing in the closet had been spared.

"Thanks anyway, Far Out," Shelly said. "Come on, Stanly, you will just have to go as you are."

Stanly glanced down at his sneakers and smiled weakly as he followed Shelly out into the hall and down to the elevator.

"You have the feeling this is going to be a long night, Stan?"

"I hope so."

The red light flickered announcing that a down elevator had arrived. The doors rattled open revealing the elevator to be as jam packed with people as usual. Stanly and Shelly crowded their way in and made the insufferable trip down with the maximum of discomfort.

As soon as they reached the bottom and were able to pry themselves loose from the walls, they made their way to the parking lot where Shelly's '57 Chevy had been stationed.

"All right, here's what we'll do," Shelly explained as they climbed inside. "First we will go to Jan's house. I'll get out there while you go pick up Tracy, then you come back and get us, and then we'll go eat?"

"You want me to get Tracy by myself?"

"I thought you wanted to see her — alone."

"I do. But you want me to drive your car, all by myself, to get her?"

"Sure."

"Shelly?"

"What?"

"I've never driven a stick shift before."

"What?"

"I've never driven a — " Stanly started.

"I heard you the first time," Shelly interrupted. "I just didn't believe it. For crying out loud, Stan!"

"I'm sorry."

"Don't be sorry, we'll just have to figure out something else, that's all."

"What?"

"Give me a second," Shelly said considering an alternate plan. "How about I leave you at Tracy's, pick up Jan, and then come back for you."

"Leave me alone at Tracy's?"

"No — she'll probably be there too."

Shelly started the car and pulled out of the campus parking lot.

"What about her parents?" Stanly asked.

"What about them?"

"What if they're there?"

"Well, I suppose they've got a right to be, it's their house."

"I mean what am I supposed to do, what am I supposed to say to them?"

"You've got to be kidding."

Shelly stopped the car. "Here we are," he said, "I'll be back in ten or fifteen minutes."

"But. . ."

"Enjoy yourself," Shelly said as he pushed Stanly out of the car. "See you in a bit."

Shelly started to pull away, then stopped and threw a small white box out the window at Stanly. "Don't forget your corsage," he called as he drove off.

Stanly got to his feet and brushed himself off, picked up the corsage and headed across the driveway toward the front door. As he started to press the doorbell he was met by a pair of slobbering, snarling fangs.

"Down Killer, down! Killer, stop it!" came David Williams' voice in sharp commands to the dog as the door was opened.

"Hi, Stan," Williams said as the dog leaped into the screen door after Stan's jugular vein.

"Back dog!" Williams said kicking the monster in the head, "I said to get back, Killer!"

The gargantuan German shepherd reluctantly retreated into the depths of the house, dissatisfied at having been deprived of a between-meal snack.

"Come on in, Stan," Williams invited. "Tracy will be out in two or three hours."

"What?"

"Just kidding, Stan," he said punching him on the arm. "Well, I'll be seeing you."

"You're leaving?"

"Jo Jo and me got plans for the night," Williams explained. "Tracy will be ready in a few minutes. Everybody else is in the TV room, you can wait for her in there if you want."

"I. . .I. . .I. . ." Stanly said.

"See you again sometime," Williams called as he departed.

As the door slammed shut, half a million little midgets crawled out of the woodwork and attacked Stanly's lower legs.

"Who are you?" asked one of the midgets.

"I'm Stanly Allen," Stanly said.

"What's your last name?"

"Allen."

"That's your first name," the midget stated.

"Stanly is my first name."

"Who cares."

"Well, I just — " Stanly started.

"I'm Tracy's mother," an extremely attractive woman said, introducing herself as she entered the room and the conversation, " and these are Tracy's little brothers and sisters. This is Sean, and Ian, and Robin, and Jason, and Christine, and Inga, and Kyle."

Stanly absorbed, digested, and instantly forgot each and every one of their names.

"So you are Stanly Allen," Mrs. Williams said.

Stanly nodded apprehensively.

"You don't look anything like what I expected."

"What did you expect?"

"Well, to tell you the truth, from what I've heard and what I've read about you, I thought you were, you know, peculiar."

"Peculiar?"

"But anyone who sees you in person can tell you're really not. In fact, I would say," Mrs. Williams stopped in mid sentence as her serveillance of Stanly reached his feet. "You are wearing sneakers," Mrs. Williams stated.

"What?"

"You are peculiar."

"Well, I — " Stanly started to explain when at that moment Tracy entered the room. Stanly took one look at her as she smiled at him, and he felt he needed to give no explanations to anyone for anything he did thereafter.

CHAPTER X

Stanly stuck the white box in front of him more on conditioned reflex than anything else.

"These are for you," he said, not able to take his eyes from that radiantly smiling face.

Tracy dug excitedly into the proffered gift.

"Oh!" she beamed happily. "Orchids, how beautiful! Aren't they beautiful! Put them on for me."

Stanly stood waiting expectantly for someone to pin the corsage on the fascinating young goddess poised in front of him, when he realized that he was the one she had been referring to.

"Me?"

"Certainly, silly, and thank you, they are beautiful. You have very good taste."

"I know," Stanly said as he took the flowers with trembling hands, and gazed nervously at the proposed target. Then with deliberate calm he gulped in a mouthful of air, withdrew three pins from the corsage, and quickly shot his hand down the front of Tracy's skin tight evening gown.

"What do you think you are doing?" Mrs. Williams asked in a level tone.

"Pinning these on," Stanly hurriedly explained as he immediately jammed all three pins into the flowers, through the dress, and into his hand.

"Ahhhhh!" Stanly screamed as he pulled his hand out of Tracy's dress.

"Ahhhhh!" Tracy cried as the pins penetrated her exposed flesh.

The unexpected jerking of Stanly's hand and Tracy's breasts, caused the corsage to drop to the floor with a dull kerfloosh.

Stanly bent down and retrieved the fallen petals. He removed the pins and started to stuff his hand down the front of Tracy's dress again, when she stopped him with a gentle touch of her hand.

"That's all right," Tracy said, "I think I can manage," she continued as she quickly and efficiently pinned the corsage above her left bosom.

"What have you got planned for tonight?" Mrs. Williams asked.

"Planned?" Stanly asked in panic.

"Yes, what have you got in mind for my daughter tonight?"

Stanly stood frozen with fear, hoping against hope that she could not read minds.

"Oh, mother," Tracy said, "really!"

Just then the United States Cavalry came riding over the hill as a car horn's blast sounded outside.

"Who is that?" Mrs. Williams asked.

"That's the cavalry," Stanly replied.

"I beg your pardon?"

"I mean that's my ride — our ride," Stanly interjected.

"Well, good night," Mrs. Williams said kissing her daughter as if it were going to be the last time she would ever see her. "Have a nice time — and be careful," she added glaring at Stanly.

"Yes, ma'am," Stanly gulped. "Good night!"

Stanly escorted Tracy to the car and quickly got her and himself inside, then sat back heavily in the seat and breathed a sigh of relief as Shelly sped away into the comforting darkness.

Things ran rather smoothly through dinner, with Shelly keeping an even flow of conversation babbling, and Stanly adding his occasional "yes, no," and "what." In fact, the only real mishap occurred when Stanly sloshed the mushroom gravy that came with the steak he ordered, down the front of his suit pants, but Shelly laughed the matter away, and didn't hit Stanly until the two girls had adjourned to the ladies room after the meal.

"Way to go, dummy," Shelly commented as he punched Stanly in the arm.

"I didn't do it on purpose," Stanly protested.

"Never mind, it doesn't matter anyway. Now when the girls get back, I'll pay for the check and you can pay me back tomorrow, then we'll go to Larry's party. All right?"

"All right."

"Stanly?"

"What?"

"Don't look now, but you see that old man over your left shoulder?"

"If I'm not supposed to look now, how could I possibly see him?"

"Don't get smart, you can look now, he's turned the other way."

"All right, I see him, so what?"

"He has been staring at us all night."

"Staring at us?"

"Well, not exactly at us, more like just Tracy."

"Why that dirty — " Stanly began starting out of his chair.

"Here come the girls," Shelly cut him off and rose to meet the approaching figures.

"Did everything come out all right?" Shelly asked with a slight grin.

"Shelly!" Jan blushed as she punched him affectionately in the stomach.

Shelly doubled over in mock pain, then unexpectedly turned up toward Stanly.

"He's coming this way," Shelly said.

"Who?"

Shelly nodded at the little man who hobbled toward them.

"Excuse me," the little man said as he sidled up close to Tracy, "but I just had to tell you how nice I think you young folks look," he said as he nonchalantly placed his gnarled little hand on Tracy's bare shoulder.

Stanly stood as quiet and still as a hand grenade resting in a bowl of oatmeal, only his eyes flared and glowed like two dark blue embers of billowing fire and rage.

"Thank you," Shelly said calmly, "Well, I think we better be going — "

"Going to the prom?" the old man questioned as his hand slid around Tracy's shoulder and down her back toward her rear proportions.

Slowly and deliberately the fingers on Stanly's right hand came together to form a neat round fist.

"Homecoming," Shelly explained as he abruptly stepped between the little old man and Tracy, forcing Tracy in between the little old man and Stanly. "Well, we've got to be going now," he continued rapidly as he took Jan by the arm, and began shepherding the others toward the front exit, making sure to always keep at least one body between Stanly's and that of the little old man.

"You girls wait here," Shelly commanded when they reached the door, "while Stanly and I go pay the bill. Come on, Stanly," Shelly said taking Stanly firmly by the arm.

"You were going to hit that old man," Shelly accused when they were out of ear shot.

"I've never hit anyone before in my entire life," Stanly replied coolly.

"You were going to hit him."

"I was going to kill him!"

"Stanly, Stanly," Shelly intoned sympathetically, "You can't kill everyone that touches Tracy or makes a pass at her."

"I don't want to kill everyone – just him."

"You can't kill anybody – what is the matter with you; what's come over you? You've never done anything like this before."

Stanly shook his head as Shelly dug out the outrageous sum for the meal they had consumed.

"I don't know," Stanly said sadly, "I don't know."

Larry Holbrook resided in Green Hall, one of the nicer dorms placed near the center of the campus for the almost exclusive use of those participating in athletic competition; the super jocks.

In answer to Shelly's knock, the door swung open to reveal a six-foot-twelve inch gorilla guarding the entrance way.

"Is Larry here?" Shelly asked.

"Inside," the gorilla grunted, jabbing his thumb at the interior of the room.

Hesitantly, the four entered the confines of the gorilla's cage.

"Wondered when you were going to get here," Larry slurred, spilling half his drink on the rug as he stumbled forward to greet them. "I almost started without you."

"Almost?" came a feminine voice from the back of the room. "You've almost finished an entire bottle of wine by yourself," Sheila continued as she came up beside Larry just in time to keep him from tipping over.

"Shhh!" Larry whispered harshly at her. "It's a secret."

"You want me to go now?" the gorilla asked.

"Yes, Rag," Sheila said.

"Where can I go?"

"Go next door and play with Sag," Sheila instructed.

"Guy," Rag mumbled as he turned to leave. "Rag deal, rag deal!"

"You've got your pet nicely trained," Shelly commented as Rag left the room.

"That's Larry's roommate, Rag," Sheila explained.

"And you sent him next door to play with Sag?" Shelly questioned.

"Rag and Sag play left guard and tackle on the football team. I don't know what their real names are. The coach nicknamed him Rag because anytime something goes wrong or something happens that he doesn't understand he says 'rag deal,' and the coach calls the other one Sag because it rhymes with Rag."

"Amazing man, that coach," Shelly offered.

"Want some wine?" Larry gurgled.

"No, I don't — " Stanly began.

"Yes, I could sure use some," Shelly stated.

"Me too," Jan added.

"So could I," Tracy said.

"How about you, Stan?" Sheila asked.

Stanly took a long heart rendering look at Tracy and gave a half smile, "Sure," he said weakly.

One hour and many drinks later, Shelly rose from his position on the floor and glanced at his watch.

"Stan," he called across the room.

Stanly's head popped up out of a drunken slumber.

"What?"

"You 'bout ready to go to the dance?"

"What dance?"

"The homecoming dance."

"Is that tonight?"

"Yup."

"I don't want to go," Stanly replied confidently as Tracy nestled her head against his shoulder.

"I don't think anybody cares whether you want to go or not." Shelly smiled drunkenly. "But Tracy has got to be there so they can crown her queen again, and take a buncha pictures."

"Oh," Stanly said as he glanced down at Tracy. "You ready to go?"

Tracy tenderly looked into Stanly's eyes, touched his lips ever so gently with her fingertips, and said in the softest breath of a whisper, "I'm drunkern a skunk."

"Yeah," Stanly said as they struggled to their feet.

"You coming?" Shelly asked Sheila.

"Sheila pointed at the prostrate figure of Larry Holbrook, wine splattered and snoring contentedly on the floor.

"Are you kidding?"

"Well, then I guess we'll be off," Shelly waved.

"Wait a minute," Sheila said as she gave Larry a swift kick in the side. "I'll get him up so he can at least say good-bye."

"Huh!" Larry snorted as he felt the pain in his side.

"They're leaving," Sheila said coldly.

"You don't have to go," Larry grinned.

"Gotta make it to the dance so Tracy can be crowned," Shelly explained.

"All right," Larry said as he staggered toward Tracy. Carefully he placed his lips next to her ear and whispered something the others were unable to hear. Tracy looked up at him, flashed a bright smile and nodded her head.

"All right," Larry said again, then toppled over backward, sprawling out on the floor where he resumed his drunken snoring.

"Good night," Shelly called.

"Good night," Sheila answered. "If you see Rag tell him he can come back in again."

Shelly glanced apprehensively at his watch as he pulled up in front of the student center ballroom.

"We've got to hurry," he said, "or Tracy is gonna miss her coronation."

"I don't care," Tracy smiled as she wrapped her arms round Stanly's neck.

"She doesn't care," Stanly repeated happily.

"Help her out of the car, Stan."

Stanly slid across the back seat, carefully dragging Tracy with him. Then he effortlessly threw open the door, and fell out of the car pulling Tracy down on top of him.

"You all right?" Stanly asked her.

"Stanly."

"Yeah?"

"I'm drunk, Stanly."

"Yeah," Stanly answered as Shelly and Jan helped them to their feet.

Once inside the crepe paper coated and dimly lit student ball room, Shelly found Tracy and Stanly two vacant seats.

"Now I want you two to sit right here. Don't move, don't do anything. Just sit right there until I find out where Tracy is supposed to be for the crowning."

"Right," Stanly saluted.

"C'mon, Jan," Shelly said taking his girlfriend by the arm, "they're too drunk to get into too much trouble."

Tracy slowly began weaving back and forth on her chair in beat to the music that filled the room. Thinking she was about to fall off her chair, Stanly quickly threw his arms about her shoulders in order to steady her.

"Stanly," Tracy said in a half breath.

As Tracy sat gazing up at him, Stanly leaned toward her, slowly, ever so slowly at first until he was no further than a fragrant whisper from her lush red lips. Tracy smiled at him and closed her eyes as Stanly's lips brushed hers. The world was summer and wine; deep and rich and. . .and suddenly a blinding flash appeared over Stanly's right shoulder.

Stanly blinked awake and instantly alert as he glanced around apprehensively.

"Thank you," the photographer said as he faded into the crowd.

"Wait!" Stanly called.

Stanly turned to Tracy.

"Tracy?" he said.

Tracy smiled at him happily, far too inebriated to even care if the world, not to mention the room, was spinning.

"Tracy?" Stanly said again.

Tracy threw her arms around Stanly's neck and smothered him with kisses.

Stanly pulled himself out of her embrace.

"Tracy!"

Tracy smiled that smile which had sent men to their doom since time began. "What?" she asked softly.

"That was a. . .he just took our. . ."

Stanly gazed into her deep emerald green eyes and shook his head sadly as her fragrant perfume overwhelmed what was left of his dulled senses, then took her in his arms and sat back resigned to accept his fate.

CHAPTER XI

"Have you seen this!" Shelly shouted as he broke into Stanly and Hiram's room waving a newspaper.

Stanly shot up in his bed and blinked away the sleep from his eyes.

"What time is it?" he asked.

"Eight o'clock."

"Eight o'clock," Stanly muttered, "in the morning?"

Stanly laid back down and turned over. "Leave me alone," he yawned.

Shelly shook Stanly roughly by the shoulder.

"What?" Stanly fought back.

"Look at this!" Shelly said as he thrust the paper in front of Stanly's face.

"Homecoming big success," Stanly read aloud.

"Would you look at the picture, stupid!"

Stanly slowly brought the picture into focus.

"Oh my God!" he ejaculated, dropping the paper as if it had suddenly burst into flames before him.

"Well, it's about time, you've finally started coming to your senses," Shelly said. "Now what are you going to do. Before, Gunther might have just roughed you up a bit, broken a few bones maybe, but now, when he sees that picture of you making it with Tracy, plastered all across the front of the paper, he'll kill you for sure."

Stanly held his head in his hands and rocked back and forth mournfully.

"Where's Hiram?" Shelly suddenly asked. "He never showed up at the dance."

Stanly looked up and shook his head.

"I don't know, he didn't come in last night, either."

The door swung open and Hiram walked in, pale and angry.

"Where have you been?" Shelly asked.

"I don't want to talk about it."

"What's the matter?"

"I don't want to talk about it, I said."

Hiram began to undress for bed.

"You wouldn't believe it," he said to himself.

"Wouldn't believe what?" Shelly asked.

"She's a lesbian."

"Who?"

"Malcolm's sister."

"What?"

"She's a lesbian."

"A lesbian?"

"That's right, a lesbian. A lesbian!"

"Are you kidding?" Shelly asked.

"Not only that, she wasn't even home when I went to pick her up."

"I know," Shelly said softly.

"I went around beating on the doors and windows of her

house for almost half an hour. Then just as I was about to leave she comes driving up with Malcolm. 'Just give me a minute and I'll be right with you,' she says, 'I want to change to a dress,' she says. It took her almost an hour to change to her dress! Then I took her to the most expensive restaurant she could find and bought her the most expensive meal on the menu. Then I finally got her back up here to the room and we had a little wine, she didn't want beer, she had to have wine, naturally. So finally, after all that, I was just about to get her into bed when she says, 'Hiram, I'm a lesbian,' just like that, 'Hiram, I'm a lesbian.' "

"What did you do?"

"I thought she was kidding! But she says, 'I thought I could pretend, but I can't. I've never met anyone like you before, but you just don't turn me on, so will you please take me home.' "

"So what did you do?"

"I please took her home."

"Then where have you been all night?"

"In the park — thinking."

"Thinking about what?"

"About what I'm going to do."

"Have you decided?"

"Yeah."

"What are you going to do?"

"Go home."

"What?"

"Go home. I'm tired of college, I'm tired of everything around here, so I'm going home."

"You can't!"

"I can, and I will," Hiram said as he climbed into bed, "I'm packing and going home tomorrow. Good night."

"Good morning," Shelly said.

"I didn't really think he would do it," Stanly said as he and Shelly watched Hiram drive out of sight.

"I did," Shelly said calmly.

"You did?" Stanly asked in amazement.

"Yeah."

"But nobody just packs up in the middle of the quarter and leaves."

"Hiram did."

"Why?"

"Because he's Hiram."

"That's not a reason."

"If Tracy all of a sudden just got up and took off for Norway, say, would you follow her?"

Stanly was silent for a while, "That's not the same thing."

"It's exactly the same. I wouldn't go after her, but I'm not Stanly Allen. I wouldn't quit college, but then I'm not Hiram Burroughs either."

"I still didn't think he'd do it," Stanly stated adamantly.

"Have you seen Tracy today?" Shelly grinned in response.

"Tracy! Oh my gosh, no!" Stanly yelled as he took off at a trot across the parking lot in the direction of the Williams' house, all thoughts of Hiram quickly fading into the distant recesses of his mind.

"Who's there?" Shelly called as the banging on his door subsided.

"It's me," came the remorseful reply.

Shelly opened the door of his room and Stanly walked in.

"What's the matter?" Shelly asked.

"She won't see me anymore."

"Tracy? Why not?"

"Gunther is coming back at the end of the week, and she's afraid that he'll hurt me."

"He'll kill you when he finds out you've been dating his girl."

"That's just it!" Stanly expostulated. "She's not his girl."

"What?"

"She has been meaning to break up with him for a long

time. They're through — but he just won't accept it."

"How do you know all this?"

"She told me last night after the dance."

"She's breaking up with Gunther, but she won't go out with you?"

"She's afraid I'll get hurt."

"You asked her for a date?"

"Uh huh."

"And she turned you down?"

"Fifteen times."

"How could she turn you down fifteen times?"

"That's what I kept asking myself, 'how could anyone turn me down fifteen times?' "

"No, I don't mean that. I mean she said no to you fifteen times?"

"I asked her for fifteen different dates."

"In one day?"

"In five minutes."

"Ask someone else for a date."

"I don't love anyone else."

"And you don't love her."

"I do!"

"I'm not going to start that again. But maybe, Stan, just maybe she doesn't love you."

"She doesn't realize how lucky she is, that's all. Anyone else who got turned down fifteen times would leave her to face Gunther all alone. But not me. No sir, not me, I'm too gallant, too honorable, too noble — "

" — too stupid."

"Too stupid," Stanly said, dropping his head to his chest.

For the next two weeks Stanly doggedly kept after Tracy for a date, and as for Tracy, she doggedly refused.

Shelly opened the door to Stanly's room, only to find himself ankle deep in papers and books that had been violently thrown to the floor.

"What happened in here?" Shelly asked.

"Two weeks!" Stanly shouted.

"What?"

"It's been two weeks since I've seen Tracy. Gunther's been back for a week now and Tracy still won't see me."

"Did Gunther do this to your room?" Shelly asked in apprehension.

"No, I did this to my room 'cause I was mad. I haven't even seen Gunther for that matter."

"I saw Larry Holbrook today."

"She's had time to tell him they're through, so why won't she see me?"

"He and Sheila have split."

"I mean if I'm going to die for her, the least she could do is go out on a date with me."

"It wasn't just because of the drugs either — it was another girl."

"What?"

"I want to talk to you, Stan," Shelly said.

"I don't want to talk," Stanly answered.

"It's about Tracy, and you, and. . ."

"What about Tracy?"

"Well," Shelly smiled sadly, "I don't really know how to tell you."

"Then don't tell me."

"I need a drink," Shelly said in desperation.

"So get one."

"What *you* need is a good stiff drink," Shelly said.

"I don't drink."

"You did when you were John Wayne."

"I still don't think that happened."

"You drank when you were with Tracy."

Stanly dropped his head, "Yeah," he said soberly.

"How about a coke then?"

"All right," Stanly consented.

Shelly placed their order for a beer and a coke at Elrod's the local 3.2 joint, then slowly nervously rocked back and forth in his chair, as Stanly sat with his elbows on the table, his chin resting on his folded hands.

"What are you thinking about?" Shelly asked as their drinks were being served.

"What do you think?"

"If you found a girl even two-thirds as good as Tracy Williams you'd forget her in a minute."

"What?"

"If you found a girl even two-thirds as good as Tracy Williams you'd forget her in a minute," Shelly repeated.

"What are you talking about?"

"Nothing. You know, I may marry Jan."

"Why?"

"Because she is mentally and physically right for me."

"Oh."

"You want to be best man?"

"No."

"Why not?"

"All right, I'll be best man."

"I don't want you to be best man if you don't want to be."

"I want to be."

They finished their drinks in silence.

"Maybe I won't marry Jan after all," Shelly said, "I've got a good thing going now, why spoil it." He glanced at Stanly, "You'll forget about Tracy in time."

"Why would I want to forget about her," Stanly asked defiantly. "What did you want to tell me about her? You brought me here to tell me something, what is it?"

Suddenly the doors opened and through the gloomy light Larry Holbrook walked in, Tracy Williams clinging to his arm and laughing gaily.

Shelly shot a quick glance at Stanly, as the two walked by without noticing them. Stanly picked up a couple of ice cubes from his glass and popped them into his mouth.

"Stanly," Shelly said, "I'm sorry, I meant to tell you about this."

"Huh?"

"About Tracy and Larry."

"You don't have to tell me."

"You want to know how it happened?"

"I think I knew it was going to happen all along, I just didn't want to believe it."

"It wasn't Larry's fault."

"It isn't anybody's fault," Stanly said, "you can't help who you fall in love with — or don't fall in love with."

"You want to go?"

Stanly dropped a couple more ice cubes in his mouth and nodded.

"I just wish I knew what I did wrong. What did I do? How did I screw it so badly?" Stanly asked the silent night as they passed outside.

"It wasn't just you. Remember that party we went to at Larry's before the dance?"

Stanly nodded.

"Well, Larry had just got in a fresh shipment of grass from California and he asked Tracy if she wanted some. So, after you took her home Saturday night she went back over to Larry's and they got high together and. . .well, they just sort of hit it off that's all."

"She takes drugs?"

"I didn't say that, I just said she smoked some grass with Larry. And what with Gunther and everything, and you, you and your high and noble ideas of love and what you're supposed to do when you're in love — you had to go and get pushy," Shelly finished.

"I'm pushy?"

Shelly didn't answer.

"I'm pushy?" Shelly repeated.

Shelly remained silent.

"I'm pushy!" Stanly shouted.

"Yes, you're pushy!"

"What do you mean I'm pushy?"

"That's what she said."

"Tracy? When?"

"When I was talking to her."

"When?"

"When I was talking to her."

"No, I mean when were you talking to her?"

"About two weeks ago, and then today when I first saw her with Larry, and they told me about everything."

"She said I was pushy?"

"Yeah."

"Me? Pushy?"

"Yes! You! Pushy! She said you kept pushing her for dates and she kept saying, 'Oh, Shelly, do something, make him quit.' "

Stanly stared into the quiet night. "Why didn't you do something?"

"I had faith in you, I thought you would come to your senses."

"Sorry I let your faith down."

"That's all right but I mean you screwed it with her but good, man."

Stanly continued to nod and stare straight ahead.

"You know I wouldn't tell you all this if I wasn't your friend?"

Stanly didn't answer.

"Don't you?"

"What?"

"You know I wouldn't tell you this if I wasn't your friend,

don't you?"

"Yeah, I know."

Stanly gazed at the darkness. He inhaled deeply. "Let's go get drunk," he said slowly expelling the air from his lungs.

CHAPTER XII

Stanly opened his eyes. His head throbbed, his throat was parched, and his stomach grumbled uncontrollably. He drew the back of his right hand across his forehead and then let it drop dejectedly back on the bed. As he did so, however, his hand brushed against something soft and warm.

Stanly painfully turned over on his right side. There, lying beside him on the bed was a strange, homely dark-haired girl, very plainly built and totally naked except for the thin blue sheet which partially draped over the lower portion of her body. Stanly watched her through blood-shot eyes for a few brief moments, her tiny round breasts gently rising and falling with each breath she took. Stanly tried to recall if he had ever seen her before, but no recollection came to his bedraggled mind.

He closed his eyes, shook his head and turned over on his back once again. Stanly forced his eyes open and looked in the direction he had last seen the drably mysterious girl, thinking, hoping, she was merely an apparition of his drunken mind. She was still there.

Stanly sat up on the bed and looked about him. He was naked, he was in his own room at the dorm, and his memory was a blank.

He got out of bed very carefully, and walked into the bathroom. A few seconds later he came back into the room wearing a green towel wrapped about his waist.

For a full minute he stood at the foot of the bed, simply staring at the sleeping figure. Then the girl gave a soft low moan and opened her eyes.

"Hello," she murmured sleepily.

Stanly continued to stare at her. "Who are you?" he finally asked.

"You don't remember?" she asked in a hurt tone.

"Remember what?"

"You really don't?"

"I'm sorry, but I guess not. What am I supposed to remember?"

"It doesn't matter!" the girl sobbed, flinging herself deep into the bed, and crying relentlessly into the pillow.

Stanly came around from the foot of the bed and sat down beside the girl. He watched her weeping form for a long confused minute.

"I'm sorry," he finally said.

He placed his hand tenderly on her bare shoulder, "Maybe if you could give me a hint."

"I'm your fiancee!"

Stanly jerked his hand away and leaped to his feet. The swift and unexpected movement unraveled the green towel so it dropped down about his ankles.

Stanly reached down to retrieve his wrapping, but as he did

so, the doorknob jiggled and then the door was flung open wide. Shelly stumbled into the room rotating an ice cube back and forth across his temples.

"Oh God, I think I'm dead, or at least dying — morning, Stan."

Stanly straightened up without recovering the towel and stared at Shelly in bewilderment.

"Something the matter, Stan?" Shelly asked.

A low simpering sob came from the bed. Stanly stood as if paralyzed by the sound. Shelly peered around Stanly's shoulder at the noise of the girl's tears, and then looked back at Stan.

"Who is she?"

"You don't remember either?" she cried.

"Don't remember what?"

The girl didn't answer.

"What don't I remember, Stan?"

The girl wiped away her tears with the back of her hand, and sat upright on the bed. Her lips quivered. "You were with him when he proposed!" she sobbed.

"Proposed? Stan, what does she mean, 'proposed'?"

"Hiram asked me to marry him," the girl answered, getting out of the bed and coming up quietly behind Stanly. "And you were going to be best man."

"Marry him?" Shelly choked.

"Is that so awful?" she sobbed again.

Stanly wheeled about so suddenly that he bumped into the girl, almost knocking her over.

"Excuse me," he apologized. "What did you say? Who asked you to marry him?"

"You did."

"No, no, that's not what you said. Who?"

"You, Hiram."

"Hold up!" Shelly said interrupting the girl, "I thought you said you were going to marry Stanly."

The girl shook her head. "Hiram."

"Hiram?" Shelly asked.

"But he's gone home," Stanly said more perplexed than ever.

Shelly ignored him.

"Where is Hiram?" he asked the girl.

She gave Shelly a quizzical look and then pointed at Stanly. Shelly turned toward Stanly and grinned broadly.

"There may be hope for you yet, Stanly, my boy." Then for the first time, Shelly seemed to notice that both Stanly and the girl were naked.

"You're going to catch cold if you run around here bare-ass like that all day," he said simply.

Stanly bent down, picked up the green towel and wrapped it around his torso. Then realizing that the girl was in the same position he had been in, Stanly unwound the towel and handed it to her. She took the towel with an expression of disbelief plainly readable upon her face, and held it up close to her body. Stanly walked into the bathroom and got another one for himself. He came out of the bathroom robed, this time, in an orange towel, and stepped toward the girl.

"My name is Stanly," he said blankly.

"What?"

"My name is Stanly, not Hiram."

"That's not possible," she said.

"What's your name?" Stanly asked the girl.

"Brenda Webb."

"Brenda," Stanly repeated, "I'm sorry about — "

Shelly grabbed Stanly around the shoulders and began dancing about the room with him. The shaky movement caused the orange towel to slip loose and drop to the floor.

"What is going on?" Brenda asked.

"Brenda, my love," Shelly said going over and wrapping his arm around her shoulders, as Stanly picked up his towel, "you will never be Mrs. Allen, or Mrs. Burroughs, but always Miss Brenda Webb."

"No," she said shaking her head and pointing to Stanly, "we were engaged last night."

"Figuratively, maybe you were. But actually, you weren't. You see, that dumb ass standing over there in that orange towel, gave you his ex-roommate's name instead of his own."

"No," she repeated. "I'm engaged to him."

" 'Fraid not."

"I'll sue!"

"Go ahead. I doubt he's got more than five dollars to his name. It would cost you more to sue than you could ever hope to get out of him. Besides there's nothing legal about an engagement. Anyway, you wouldn't want to marry a guy who won't even tell you his real name, would you?"

Brenda dropped her towel, rushed over, and threw her arms around Stanly's neck. Stanly barely managed to keep a desperate hold on his own towel.

"Didn't you enjoy last night?" she asked confidently.

"I don't know," Stanly said shaking his head sadly.

"What?"

"I don't remember."

"Not even the chandelier — the poodle — the window?"

Stanly gave her a blank look.

Brenda pushed herself away from Stanly.

"You bastard!"

"Now there's no need to get nasty," Shelly said.

"Go to hell! Both of you!"

"Yes, ma'am," Shelly said, "I expect he's already there, and I'm sure working on it."

"I'll sue!" Brenda repeated, rushing out of the room and into the hall,

"I'll go talk to her," Shelly shouted, picking up the green towel and racing after her.

Stanly shook his head sadly, walked into the bathroom and threw up.

Two hours later Shelly returned to Stanly's room carrying a green towel under his arm and a magazine in his hand. Stanly was dressed, and standing in front of the mirror in the bathroom looking at the redness and swelling of his eyes.

"I got it all straightened out," Shelly said laying the magazine and the towel down on Stanly's desk. "She's not going to sue you if you will pay her for damages."

Stanly stepped out of the bathroom.

"We sure must have had some night," Shelly continued, "according to her anyway. Want to hear about it?"

Stanly shook his head.

"Sure you do," Shelly said.

"No."

"Aren't you even the least bit curious?"

"No."

"Not even about the chandelier or the poodle or the window? Those are the damages you are going to have to pay for if you want to keep her from suing you."

"What?"

"I thought that might arouse your interest. What's the last thing you remember about last night?"

"Going into some bar."

"Well, we went into five before my memory gave out. After that I'm not sure what happened till we got to Jan's house."

"Jan's house?"

"That's where you met Brenda."

"Brenda's a friend of Jan's?"

Shelly shook his head, "Her cousin."

"Oh, God," Stanly said, and dropped his head into his hands. "What happened at Jan's house?"

"Nothing."

"Nothing?"

"All the action took place at Brenda's house."

"Brenda's house?" Stanly repeated.

Shelly nodded, "We just stayed at Jan's house long enough

to drink up all her dad's liquor. Then Brenda said that there was plenty of booze over at her house, so that's where we went."

Shelly paused for effect.

"What happened?" Stanly choked.

"Then we had an orgy," Shelly said simply.

Stanly jerked his head up, "Just the two of us?"

"There were four of us; you and Brenda, and me and Jan."

Stanly shook his head and dropped it back into his hands, "What about the chandelier?"

"Well, it seems that Brenda had this big chandelier hanging in the middle of her living room — "

"Had?"

"You broke it."

"How?"

"That's where you were doing it with Brenda."

"Up in the chandelier?"

Shelly nodded, "But it broke."

"The chandelier?"

Shelly nodded again.

"Was anyone hurt?"

"Only her poodle."

"Her poodle?"

"She had this little black poodle and it was standing under the chandelier when it broke."

"Did it hurt him?"

"Not then."

"Not then?"

"No, you only scared him, but he started running around the house yelping. That's when you picked him up and threw him through the window."

"Oh, God," Stanly said shaking his head.

"I think that's when you hurt him."

Stanly continued to shake his head and moan.

"But it's all right," Shelly said.

"All right?" Stanly echoed.

"She didn't like the dog anyway. So if you'll just pay for the chandelier, the poodle, and the window, she will forget about the law suit; unless she gets pregnant that is," Shelly added.

"Pregnant! You don't think she'll get pregnant, do you?"

Shelly shook his head, "No, she was too drunk to get pregnant."

"Too drunk! What has being drunk got to do with being pregnant?"

"Nothing really, but I thought it might ease your mind if I said it."

"You think Jan will get pregnant?"

"No. We've been balling off and on for the last year. She's on the pill."

Stanly shook his head remorsefully. "Oh, God," he said, "Why? Why, why, why?"

"It's not really that bad."

Stanly stared at Shelly in disbelief.

"Well, think of the knowledge aspect, Stanly."

"What knowledge aspect?"

"What you learned from it," Shelly replied cheerfully. "You did learn from it, didn't you? That's the important thing — what you learned from it."

Stanly glared mutely at Shelly.

"You do think that's the important thing, don't you?"

Stanly dropped his vision to the floor.

"You're going to hit me aren't you?"

"No," Stanly said quietly.

"You're not?"

"No," Stanly repeated.

"Why not?"

"What good would it do?"

"Maybe you would feel better."

"Maybe."

"You sure you don't want to hit me?"

"I'm sure."

"Maybe just one little poke on the chin."

"No."

"As your friend, I think you should hit me."

"I don't want to hit you."

"I insist."

"Go to hell," Stanly said softly, and walked out of the room.

CHAPTER XIII

"Stanly!" Shelly called after him.

"What?"

"Where are you going?"

"I don't know."

Stanly left the dorm with Shelly at his heels, and strolled aimlessly through the campus grounds.

"I'm going to go home tomorrow for Thanksgiving," Shelly said. "You want to come home with me?"

"No."

"You're not staying here because of Tracy are you?"

Stanly glanced up at the colorless gray sky.

"Damnit," he said. "November twentieth and no snow. This is going to be one hell of a shitty Christmas."

"You still love her don't you?" Shelly said.

Stanly didn't answer.

"You'll get over it. You can get over anything eventually. It's a state of mind, you know — God, I hope Jan remembers to take her pill."

"What?"

"I hope Jan remembers her pill."

"What pill?"

"Her birth control pill."

"Oh."

"If she doesn't take it she becomes twice as fertile the next day, you know."

"I didn't know."

"What?"

"I didn't know she became twice as fertile."

Shelly nodded, "Maybe I should call her."

"Why?"

"To remind her to take her pill. If even half the things Brenda said we did last night are true, then she's going to need to take her pill."

"Call her," Stanly said.

Shelly shook his head. "No, I trust her. Besides, if she gets pregnant it's her own fault."

Stanly stuck his hands deep into his pockets.

"Have you ever noticed a dog's eyes from the side, Stan?" Shelly asked.

"What?"

"Have you ever noticed a dog's eyes from the side?"

"Well, it sorta blends together, the white and the cornea. Now people's corneas stick out from the white, but a dog's just sorta blends right into the white.

"You know, I've really learned a lot about anatomy since I've been going with Jan. Especially women's anatomy. Before I went with her, I used to think that I knew quite a bit, but I was really ignorant about it — Stanly?"

"What?"

"Never marry a virgin, Stanly. Virgins are so inexperienced.

They don't know anything sexual. They don't know any of the moves; and there's a lot of good moves. You know what I think?"

"What?"

"I think that people have the wrong attitude about sex and love. They think that you have to have a super fine body or a super fine mind before anything can work out. That's not true. Take Jan and me for instance. She has a nice body, but it's not super fine, and she has a good mind, but it's not overly intelligent. She is just right for me. It's a combination of both.

"I'd never marry a virgin. Jan wasn't a virgin when I started going with her. You see, Stan, you can't know only what a person's mind is like, and then marry them. It just wouldn't work out. You've also got to know whether they are sexually right for you.

"Say if Jan had a hole this big," Shelly said placing his thumb and index finger together to form a circle about the size of a nickel, "we'd never make it, no way. We could love each other's minds all to pieces, but it just wouldn't work out. Sex is fifty percent of the whole deal, and sex is like anything else; experience is knowledge. So I say this to you, Stanly Allen, go out and get a little knowledge."

"What?"

"Go out and get a little knowledge, Stanly. Forget about Tracy and Larry. Maybe you and her were just never meant to be. There are lots of other girls. Date them all, not just one type of girl either, but all kinds. Prudes, whores, prostitutes — did you know that I once had a prostitute, Stan?"

"No."

"I did. I'm not ashamed of it. It was knowledge, Stan, and I learned from it. Sexually it wasn't worth the ten dollars — she had a hole this big," he said putting his hands together to form a circle about the size of a basketball, "and I slopped all around. But as for knowledge, it was worth far more than the ten. You know what I'm trying to say, Stan?"

"I know," Stanly said.

"Well?"

"Well what?"

"What do you think?"

"I'm hungry," Stanly said scratching the tip of his nose. "Let's get something to eat."

They walked to the campus parking lot in silence. Shelly's '57 Chevy was the only car left on the grounds. They climbed in, Stanly buckled his seat belt, and then looked at Shelly.

"Where to?" Shelly asked as he started the engine.

"I don't care."

Shelly backed the Chevy out of the parking lot and drove to an obscure hamburger joint a few blocks away.

"This place all right?"

"Fine."

They got out of the car and entered the drive in. Shelly ordered a cheeseburger, french fries, and a coke, and went to a table to wait for Stanly while he made his order. A few minutes later Stanly came over to the table with a hamburger in one hand and a coke in the other, and sat down.

"Want some of my french fries, Stan?"

"No."

Stanly unwrapped the paper from around the hamburger, and then removed the top bun. He quickly picked all the pickles out and handed them to Shelly.

"Thanks."

"You're welcome."

Stanly replaced the top bun and bit into the hamburger.

"This tastes shitty."

"Want some french fries to go with it?"

"No."

Stanly chewed on his hamburger in utter silence.

"You sure?"

"I'm sure."

They lapsed into an unbroken silence for five minutes, and

then Shelly pointed out the window. "Hey, look out there," he said.

Stanly turned at Shelly's gesture and glanced out the window as a coal black Edsel pulled into the parking lot.

"That's Gunther's car, isn't it?" Shelly asked.

"I don't know," Stanly mumbled.

Mike Gunther withdrew his giant hulk from his car and entered the diner. He ordered a small lunch and then took a table across from Stanly and Shelly. Stanly gulped down the rest of his hamburger and hurriedly finished off his coke.

"Want a french fry?" Shelly asked.

"No."

Stanly stared long and hard at Gunther's back.

Shelly cleared his throat. "Want to go?"

"No," Stanly said calmly.

Shelly turned slightly in his chair so that he had an unobstructed view of Gunther's back. He whistled softly, "He's an animal isn't he, Stan?"

Stanly continued to stare at Gunther's back.

"You know, it's really kind of funny, Stan," he said. "You went through all that mental agony, worrying about when Gunther was going to kill you, and it ends up he probably doesn't even know who you are. There he is sitting at that table next to ours, and he doesn't even know who you are.

"Don't you think it's kind of funny, Stan? Here you were, ready to give up your life for Tracy. You were all ready to fight Gunther for her, and let him kill you. And then she turns around and drops you and him and he doesn't even know about you.

"All that nobleness, that gallantry, that chivalry gone to hell. Don't you think that's kind of funny, Stan?"

Stanly slowly got up from the table without a word, and crossed over to where Gunther was sitting.

"Stan? Where you going, Stan?" Shelly called to him.

Stanly tapped Gunther on the back of the shoulder.

"Yeah?" Gunther asked looking up.

"You are a bastard," Stanly said quietly, bringing his right fist up and catching Gunther a blow on his exposed chin.

Gunther toppled backwards out of his chair, and heavily hit the floor. Shelly leaped to his feet, and rushed toward Stanly.

"My God!" he muttered under his breath. "He's insane!"

Shelly reached Stanly's side just as Gunther started to rise to his feet. Shelly took the situation in at a glance, and taking decisive action, he turned around and hit Stanly squarely on the jaw. Stanly dropped to the floor like a pile of rubble.

"I'm sorry about my friend," Shelly apologized as he rushed over and helped Gunther to his feet. "He didn't mean it, he's drunk."

"If that son-of-a-bitch ever comes in here again — "

"He won't," Shelly assured him.

Shelly crossed back to where Stanly was spread out on the floor, bent down and got a good hold under Stanly's armpits, and then half dragged — half carried him out to the car. Shelly then climbed in behind the wheel, started the motor, and drove away from the diner and Gunther.

Stanly slowly opened his eyes, and tenderly began to rub his chin.

"It's a good thing you were smart enough to stay down when I hit you," Shelly said.

Stanly continued to massage his chin in silence.

"My God, what got into you? Why did you hit him anyway?"

"It seemed like the thing to do at the time."

"He could have killed you!"

"I know."

"That's why I hit you, you know."

"I know."

"You hit him pretty damn good," Shelly grinned at the thought.

"Yeah," Stanly said somberly.

"You know what I think?"

"No."

"I think you ought to go out and get another girl."

"You're right," Stanly said without emotion.

"What?"

"You're right."

"You mean you're going to get another girl? You're going to forget about Tracy? After all that suffering? Why?"

"Take me back to the dorm."

Shelly directed the car, in compliance with Stanly's request, and in a matter of minutes he was pulling into the vacant parking lot. Shelly quickly parked in one of the empty slots and turned off the motor.

Stanly got out of the car and headed for the dorm, followed closely by Shelly.

"So, you're going to forget about her," Shelly said.

"What?"

"So, you're going to forget about her," Shelly repeated.

"Who?"

"Tracy."

"No — I don't think so. I don't think I'll ever see her again, but I doubt I'll ever forget her."

"You're just going to give her up? Why? I don't understand. You just hit Gunther and now you're going to give her up."

"You were right."

"About what?"

"I screwed it with her. At the first I might have had a chance, but I screwed it. It's over, that's all."

Shelly shook his head. "If you had it to do all over again, you'd do it exactly the same way, wouldn't you? You'd make the same mistakes, and go through the same suffering wouldn't you?"

"Probably," Stanly said.

They were silent for a long minute.

"Want to go drinking tonight?" Shelly asked.

"Sure," Stanly said as they entered his room.

"Jan has this friend that she works with, a fine broad, really, not like Brenda."

"Fine."

"I'm glad you've finally come to your senses, Stanly. By the way," Shelly continued, "you got a magazine today. They put it in my mail box by mistake so I brought it over here and left it on the desk. It's under that towel."

Stanly lifted the towel up and picked the magazine off the desk. He glanced at the photograph on the cover and then slowly flipped through the pages one by one. Suddenly, two small white envelopes slipped out from between two of the leaves and floated to the floor.

"What's that?" Shelly asked.

Stanly picked the envelopes up off the floor and slit the first one open. He quickly pulled the letter out, unfolded it, and skimmed over the neatly typed words.

"Who's it from?" Shelly asked.

"The president of the school. He says I'll have to leave because of my grades." Stanly opened the second letter.

"That one any better news?" Shelly questioned. "Who's it from?"

"The President of the United States."

"The President?"

"I've been drafted."

"What?"

"Yeah," Stanly said softly.

524-00109-100

Stop It! I Love It!
by Laurence Schwab
and
Karen Markham

If you are one of the 40 million women who find themselves inhibited, hung-up and unable to express their sexuality, then this book is for you.
$1.00

524-00111-100

Discover Your Sexual Personality
by Laurence Schwab
and
Karen Markham

Here is a complete Sexual Analysis program for you or anybody about whom you would like to know the real truth. Are you hot stuff or maybe a cold fish.
$1.00

524-00116-095

Prisoners Of Devil's Claw
by Edward Hawkins

An epic saga told against the breathtaking background of the Rocky Mountains. Al Palmer sets out on a one man mission to rescue 2000 Union soldiers held by a demented former Southern officer.

$.95

524-00101-095

Wellspring
by Edward Hawkins

Exciting, suspenseful reading about the horrible impending death of 40,000,000 Americans as the result of an unthinkable foreign power plot. This is the book which the Pentagon wishes had never been written. It's a book which will keep you awake long after you have finished reading it.

$.95

524-00121-125

Astrology for Men
and
Astrology for Women

Two books written to show why people with the same sun signs are different because of sex and/or moon sign.

Since many persons have previously been unaware of the importance of the Moon in their horoscope, they are also unaware of their Moon sign. Miss von Ifft has therefore developed a set of charts which provides an easy and simple method for you to determine Sun-Moon signs for yourself and your friends.

$1.25 each

524-00122-125

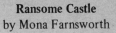

Ransome Castle
by Mona Farnsworth

Aunt Dierdre sought a home that would be appropriate. Meg Stuart, her niece, was an invited guest. So starts this haunting tale of screaming, panic, and blood chilling fear.

$.95

524-00103-095

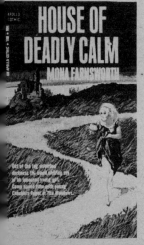

The House of Deadly Calm
by Mona Farnsworth

Young Checkers Paget liked nice old Mrs. Roderick. Poor Checkers, how was she to know. And there was Cynthia, more beautiful than any breathing mortal has a right to be. A tale to chill the heart of the most avid mystery reader.

$.95

524-00106-095

524-00110-095

The Agent Orange Affair
by James L. Watson

A nameless horror founded in secret scientific government research. Dr. Robert Marsh is pitched into a super power struggle to develop and deploy the ultimate destructive weapon.
$.95

524-00112-095

Beware of the Cat
by Roger Sherman

What happens when tolerance ends and one man decides that he's had enough of the spoiled young hippie kids? Its message is clear. It speaks of today. A book for everyone, young and old alike.

$.95

524-00118-095

The Seeker
by William Maidment

One man's mind bending search for love. Somewhere, someplace Don Rains would find his perfect woman, but before then would he destroy himself searching? How much can one man take, how many women, how many blurred memories?

$.95

524-00108-095

The Adulteress
by William Maidment

Deep in every man's mind is the question of his wife's faith. Bill Wentworth discovered the agonizing truth. Mrs. Sandra Elliston Wentworth was young, blonde and excitingly beautiful... A good look at sex in suburbia.

$.95

524-00104-125

Behold the Upright
by Ferd Nauheim

Here at last a battleground classic transcending anything you have ever read before. Come spend a war with young Sgt. Ed Gammon. Full of sound, fury and emotion — A truly great novel.

$1.25

524-00119-100

You Can Defend Yourself
by Anthony Cillo
Richard Garner
Patrick Going

A realistic approach to defending you and your loved ones from prowlers, hecklers, rapists, purse-snatchers, and the like. Prepared and fully illustrated by the three head unarmed combat instructors at the U.S. Air Force Academy.

$1.00

ORDER FORM
APOLLO BOOKS

Astrology and Occult

- [ ] *EVERYONE'S COMPLETE ASTROLOGY
  AND HOROSCOPE,Rebecca von Ifft $1.50
- [ ] MYSTIC SCIENCES, Margaret Waite 1.00
- [ ] ASTROLOGY FOR WOMEN ONLY
  Rebecca von Ifft 1.25
- [ ] ASTROLOGY FOR MEN ONLY
  Rebecca von Ifft 1.25

Non-Fiction

- [ ] STOP IT! I LOVE IT! L. Schwab and K. Markham . . . 1.00
- [ ] DISCOVER YOUR SEXUAL PERSONALITY,
  L. Schwab and K. Markham 1.00

References

- [ ] *DOCTOR'S HANDBOOK FOR PARENTS,
  the Complete and Comprehensive Encyclopedia
  of Child Care and Development 1.50
- [ ] YOU CAN DEFEND YOURSELF
  Maj. Richard B. Garver
  Lt. Col. Anthony R. Cillo
  Capt. Patrick E. Going 1.00

Cookbooks

- [ ] YOU DON'T HAVE TO BE JEWISH TO BE A GOOD COOK,
  Katheryn Winer & Lois Levine 1.00

Mystery and Suspense

- [ ] WELLSPRING, Edward Hawkins 95
- [ ] PRISONERS OF DEVIL'S CLAW, Edward Hawkins 95
- [ ] THE AGENT ORANGE AFFAIR, James Watson 95
- [ ] THE ACCIDENTAL SPY, James Watson 95

General Fiction

- [ ] RAIN FOR A DUSTY SUMMER, Margaret Waite 95
- [ ] BEWARE OF THE CAT, Roger Sherman 95
- [ ] THE ULTIMATE WEAPON, Anthony Palange 95
- [ ] THE ADULTERESS, William Maidment 95
- [ ] THE SEEKER, William Maidment 95

War Novels

☐ **BEHOLD THE UPRIGHT**, Ferd Nauheim 1.25
☐ **EXIT WITH DRUMS**, Joseph A. Daley 1.25

Gothic Novels

☐ **HOUSE OF DEADLY CALM**, Mona Farnsworth 95
☐ **RANSOME CASTLE**, Mona Farnsworth 95

Expose

☐ **THE BEAUTIFUL PEOPLE**, J.D. Russell 95

Please enclose an additional 10 cents for postage and handling.
*Please enclose an additional 15 cents for postage and handling.

Mail with check or money order to:
APOLLO BOOKS
30 Hazel Terrace
Woodbridge, Connecticut 06525

Name_____

Address _____

City _____ State _____

Zip Code_____

524-00135-095